Don't Shoot Your Mule

Also by Beth Duke:

Delaney's People: A Novel In Small Stories

Don't Shoot Your Mule

Beth Duke

Print ISBN: 978-1475102253

The Art of Dixie

Cover Photo: "Radar"
Courtesy of Paul and Donna Kadle

Author Photo by Jay Duke

Acknowledgments

Everything I write is for my mother, Patricia Poucher. I believe we all go through life trying to produce things for mommy to hang on the refrigerator and this book is no exception. Thank you for instilling a love of reading and language as well as encouraging my imagination to soar. How could I *not* be a writer?

My first novel, *Delaney's People*, opened up a new world for me. Hearing from those who read it and grew to love Delaney, her family and friends as much as I was a great joy. Your daily requests for a sequel have been answered, and I pray you'll enjoy it.

I continue to be blessed with phenomenal friends, many of whom I've known for years and some recently added through my writing. Their support has been invaluable, especially that of my "early readers" Beth Monette, Savannah Duke, and Debbie Tuckerman. Thank y'all for poring over the words and giving me feedback.

David "Papa" Boyd purchased the first copy of *Delaney's People* and reserved the first of this book, too. He has been a wonderfully enthusiastic fan and promoter of my writing. The same is true of Margaret Higgins Pendley, who also served as a resource about the world of accounting. Dave White came up with the perfect song when I could not name a tune. Add to these folks the countless others who were kind enough to attend book signings and tell me they could not wait to see what happens next . . . your words were more inspirational than you know.

Mike Cheston and Taylor Dial, thank you for your insights.

Dr. Jacqueline Tessen is the best OB/Gyn in the world and provided much useful and appreciated information.

Paul and Donna Kadle are the finest cousins and mule consultants an author could ask for.

Jay Duke and Jason Duke, thank you for believing in me and honoring my endless pleas for silence. My darling Savannah, your enthusiasm and smile light every step of this journey. I love you, family.

For Mamas

My dearest Delaney,

When you were eight years old a friend told me,

"As long as your great-granddaughter walks this

Earth, you will be here. She is so much like you."

It was the greatest compliment of my life.

I hope you have learned from me as much as I

have from you.

May God bless you in every way.

Remember always how very much I love you,

Mama D.

Tears in a Bottle

Delaney (age eleven and a half), 2011

Mama D. gave me an antique pink glass perfume bottle with a rhinestone stopper when I was a little girl. She filled it with honeysuckle cologne, using the teeniest funnel in the world. I put honeysuckle on my wrists every day of first grade, and remember thinking that Michael Fulmer liked me better because I smelled good. We held hands on the playground when no one was looking.

By second grade, I was receiving marriage proposals from Michael's cousin Gary, even though I was out of honeysuckle. Mama D. said I was beautiful, but that was not the only reason for boys to like me. She told me, "Delaney, you are smart and funny and you have the kindest heart in the world. Everyone loves you almost as much as I do."

Today I was using the bottle for the most important reason I could imagine. After the grown-ups got through hugging and telling me that Mama D. was in a better place, and she was very proud of me, and that I look like her—the bottle and I were going to the upstairs bathroom at church.

It was in my Hello Kitty purse all through the service, and I kept taking it out and turning it over in my hands. Mom didn't say anything like she usually does when I play with stuff during the sermon. She kept her arm around Daddy and left me alone.

After Brother Roy finally stopped talking and we sang every single verse of *How Great Thou Art*, my great-aunt Sarah Anne was the first person to come up to me. Her charm bracelet got tangled in my hair, but she didn't notice. "Delaney," she said, "Your great-grandmother thought you were the most lovely thing she had ever laid eyes on. She still does. She is in Heaven watching over you."

I didn't know if that was true. I felt really sick, and my dress was too tight. I only wanted to escape all the people who were trying to make me feel better. I did not want to feel better.

The bathroom had old pink tiles and it was always cold in there. The ladies from the church kept flowers next to the sink. They were purple today, and I thought they looked cheap and ugly. Mama D. would have thought the same thing.

I opened the stall door as quietly as I could and prayed that no one would come looking for me. I knew Mom and Daddy would be standing in line talking to everyone for a while. I flipped the little wire to pop the bottle open and held it next to my nose. Then I cried. I let all my tears fill it up, back and forth between my eyes. One tear at a time, I was able to catch enough to come to the very top. I patted the rhinestone stopper into place and wrapped the pink glass in toilet paper. This is how I would keep the worst day of my life with me—in a tiny, secret bottle. I promised Mama D., "I will always think of you, and try to make you proud of me. I will hear your voice telling me right from wrong. I will be the biggest part of you left behind."

I heard the bathroom door whoosh open and spotted Katy

Jackson's black high heels in front of the sink. She was thirteen and her parents let her wear tons of make-up and have a Facebook, something Mom would not even talk about. I tried to be very still as she primped and fluffed her brown-with-pink-streaks hair. It was blond two weeks ago. The last thing I wanted to do was have a conversation with Katy, so naturally, she saw my shoes and knocked on my stall door. "Are you all right, Delaney?" Nice to know she paid attention to my stupid-looking black patent flats. Even worse, Mom made me wear itchy stockings with them.

"I'm fine, thank you." I stepped into her cloud of Britney Spears perfume, tugging on the front of my dark green dress. My fingers went unconsciously to the little rhinestone brooch I had near my left shoulder. It was Mama D.'s. "Are there still lots of people here?"

"Most of them have gone on to your great-grandmother's house, I think." Katy pulled a tube of Great Lash from her Coach bag and flicked her lashes twice in the mirror. "I will walk down with you. I know you have been through a lot today." The next thing I knew, I had a black-lace-covered arm tightly squeezing my shoulders, propelling me toward the hall. I wanted to hit her so bad. I bent over to brush something off my knee so I could break away.

"Did you know my great-grandmother, Katy?" I asked, tilting my head to one side. I already knew the answer.

"I never met her, Delaney, but I am sure she was a nice lady." A nice lady.

"She was, Katy, but much more than that. She was everything to me. I could talk to her about anything. She believed in me like no one else does. She had more taste and style in her little finger than all the people in this church combined. And to be honest, she would probably tell me that you are the kind of girl who wears too much make-up and I should not hang around with you."

Katy froze. I waited thirty seconds for her to form a response, then headed for the stairs alone.

I only felt a tiny bit bad about slapping Katy with words instead of my palm. I hated pretty much everyone that day and only wanted to be alone in my room at home. I decided to tell Mom I had a stomachache so I could escape the fifteen course meal that would be waiting on Mama D.'s dining room table. When someone dies in The South, every neighbor within twenty miles experiences a casserole reflex. You could bet a million dollars there would be banana pudding, too. I was hurrying so fast I missed the last step and stumbled a little, right into the shoulder of Katy's brother Chris. He was standing in the hall reading posters. His hands were jammed into the pockets of a dark blue hoodie. Katy was a real pain, but Chris was the cutest boy I had seen in my life. I'd spent over a year watching the back of his head from our pew on Sundays. He did not know I existed, and it was embarrassing to introduce myself by collision. Would this day ever end?

Either Chris did not feel my bowling ball head smack him, or he was too nice or shy or whatever to turn my way. He kept studying the poster for some Christian band that would be playing in Gadsden so I could exit gracefully. As if.

Mom and Daddy were standing with Lily and Millard, the only black people in the building. They had their own church a few miles away but would not have missed being there for my Daddy today. Even though Lily was old, I was taller than her. It was awkward when she put her arms around me because I was used to grown-ups reaching down. It felt really good, though. Lily was one of the nicest people in my life. She's kind of like a sister to my Granddaddy and aunt to my dad.

"Are y'all going to the graveyard?" Lily asked Daddy, stroking the back of my head.

"No, we're heading straight for her condo. We'll go over there later. I'm just not up for it right now."

Lily smiled at Daddy with the warmth of a thousand fireplaces in winter. "I understand, Tommy. We will see y'all there."

Mom grabbed my hand and we started down the endless steps in front of First Baptist. The sun was blinding. It seemed so wrong for it to shine today. If I had my way about it, the skies would be cloudy and gray, without a single bird singing.

As we were pulling out of our parking space, Chris Jackson ran up to Daddy's window and tapped it. Daddy rolled it down. "I think this fell out of your daughter's purse," he said, handing over a wad of toilet tissue.

Daddy nodded and said, "Thank you, Chris." Without a word he passed the tiny bundle over his seat back to me. Inside was my perfume bottle, unbroken and still full. It must have fallen out when I plowed my graceful way into Chris's back. Neither Mom or Daddy even looked to see what I had, as though lost wads of toilet paper were returned as precious treasure every day. I tucked it in under my wallet, determined to hide it safely in my underwear drawer the minute we got home.

It took about fifteen minutes to get to her place. The car was completely silent all the way, with Mom staring out her window and Daddy concentrating on driving. I reached into my Hello Kitty bag five times to make sure the bottle was still there.

I wanted to scream when we drove up, because there were at least twenty cars parked in front of Mama D.'s. Twenty cars full of people who wanted to tell me how lucky I was to have had my great-grandmother. Twenty cars full of back and head pats, hair strokes and hugs. Twenty cars full of "she is in a better place." Twenty cars of the worst way I could spend the rest of this day.

When we got inside I said, "Mom, my stomach hurts. I am going into Mama D.'s room to lie down." She hugged me and whispered, "Find me if you need anything, baby."

Her bed smelled just like her, and it was hard to believe I would not see her in it again. I walked over to her closet, where Mama D. and I had looked at jewelry together a thousand times. It was all there, in seven big boxes—sparkling, beautiful rhinestones and crystals. I opened one and found her necklaces pinned to black velvet boards, arranged by color. The first necklace was blue, so I put it on and looked in her bathroom mirror. My great-grandmother's face looked back at me, smiling and young and happy. I remembered when Daniel, Lily's son, had died years ago. Mama D. used her jewelry to explain to me how your body may be gone, but the beautiful things about you live forever on Earth, in the hearts of the people who loved you. Her perfume was on the counter. I dabbed a little on my wrists and headed out to see the family and friends who came to comfort us, knowing that Margaret Dawson Parker Duncan was walking out with me.

Her tiny living room was crammed with people sitting with plates on their laps. I couldn't find my mom anywhere, but my cousin Michael spotted me and elbowed his way over. "Hi, Laney," he said. "I am sorry about your great-grandmother."

"Thank you, Michael." I scanned the hallway for an escape route and was stunned to see Chris Jackson and his dad talking to my great-aunt Sarah Anne. What were they doing here? My first thought was to run back to Mama D.'s room, except it was too late. Chris saw me and walked over with his right hand extended to shake.

Well, this was awkward. I shook his hand in the most ladylike manner I could imagine and smiled, hoping my eyes weren't too red. "Thank you for returning my perfume bottle."

His hands disappeared into his pockets and he shrugged. "No problem," he muttered to the floor.

"Delaney!" I heard my mother's voice, but couldn't see her anywhere. "Excuse me, Chris," I said. "No problem," was his eloquent reply.

When I found Mom, she was in the kitchen looking very upset. "What's the matter?" I asked.

"Your Grandma Ellen is not feeling very well, and your daddy went with her to the hospital. I am sure she is fine, honey, but I think we should go over there."

"Just let me grab my purse," I said, and made my way through the forest of people to Mama D.'s bedroom. I was wondering what else could possibly go wrong in my world today when I banged my shin on her footboard on the way out. I had no more tears to cry, though. I guess everyone had heard about Grandma, because the group parted like the Red Sea as I entered the hall. Their faces were solemn and grave. Mrs. Wilson, my old Sunday School teacher, grabbed and hugged me. "Be brave, Delaney."

"Yes, ma'am."

Granddaddy had already gone to the hospital, so it was just Mom and me in the car. Neither of us said anything until we got to the parking lot. "Where is a freaking parking space?" Mom glared and spun the car around a corner. I was not about to add to her problems, so I sat still and silent as she missed a Ford truck's trailer hitch by an inch. We ended up a mile or so from the emergency room's entrance.

I know no one likes hospitals, but visiting one right after a funeral is absolutely the worst. We walked into the waiting room and went straight to the information desk. The nurse said, "She is with her son and husband right now. Are you family?"

"Yes, I am her daughter-in-law," Mom replied. "Please, where is she?"

Mom has a tendency to look like a horse in a barn fire when she is stressed out.

The nurse gave us a calm, reassuring look and told her, "Follow me. The doctor hasn't seen her yet. She is behind a curtain back here."

Daddy and Granddaddy were standing shoulder to shoulder, hiding our view of Grandma's bed. Mom tapped Daddy lightly and he turned around and swept her up in his arms. "They're waiting for an ECG update," he said.

Grandma waved her hand at me from the top of the white blanket. They had her tightly tucked in.

"Hi, Grandma," I said as I walked over. "Are you okay?"

"Of course I am, Delaney. This is all very silly. It has been a rough day and I was feeling faint, so your Granddaddy made me come here." She stuck her tongue out at him. I figured that was a good sign.

I tried to decide the best way to steer the conversation. I was still wearing Mama D.'s necklace and afraid that mentioning it would make things worse. Grandma reached over and stroked the blue crystals. "She wore this to my high school graduation," she sighed and smiled gently, "and I hadn't seen it since. I am worried about you, baby. I know how much you miss her already."

Well, that did it. I buried my head next to her neck and started to cry just as the doctor walked in. "Mrs. Robinson?" he asked. When she nodded I stood up and backed away.

"All of your tests look good. We can keep you overnight for observation if you'd like, but I think you are okay to go home."

That was it? That was the best they could do for my grandmother? "Excuse me," I said, "is her ECG normal?" I know he thought I was a stupid kid, but it seemed like someone should speak up.

"Who are you, darlin'?" he grinned and asked.

I hate it when grown-ups give you the equivalent of a head pat without even reaching over. "I am her granddaughter, Delaney Robinson." I reached out a hand to shake.

"Well, you are mighty mature for your age, aren't you, Delaney? Yes, her ECG is fine, and so is the blood work we did. Are there any tests you'd like to order?"

I couldn't tell if he was being an ass or really wanted to sound kind and professional. I shook my head no.

"Are you planning to be a doctor, Miss Delaney?"

"Actually, I think I might want to be. Either that or a writer. Mama D. says . . . said . . . I would be great at either one."

"Is this your Mama D.?"

Wow, wrong question. Five pairs of eyes turned to him in unison. "No sir, my Mama D.'s funeral was this morning."

"I am so very sorry," he said to the group. I was embarrassed for him. He reached up and rubbed a bald spot on the top of his head. "Well, Mrs. Robinson, I am going to release you, but I would like for you to see your regular doctor within three or four days, all right?

The nurse will give you written instructions. Just take it very easy for me." He nodded at each of us and turned to leave. "Delaney, I hope you do study medicine some day. I think you may have a terrific bedside manner." He flashed a grin at me. "Your grandma here is doing well, but keep an eye on her for me and call if you feel it's necessary." He handed me a business card and left.

Grandma Ellen said, "If all of you would kindly allow me to gather my dignity and clothes, I would like to get out of here." I could tell by her spunky tone that she was feeling like herself again.

Mom offered, "Ellen, let me help you."

Grandma replied, "No, Lisa, I am fine. All y'all need to go out in the hall. I won't fall."

"Grandma, you sound like Dr. Seuss." I winked at her.

"I used to date him, Delaney."

"Did you for real?" I asked, wide eyed.

"No, Squirt. He was much too old for me. Too goofy, too. I needed someone deeply serious like Tom Robinson."

Granddaddy rolled his eyes.

When we got into the hall, we saw Lily and Millard waiting on a couch across from the nurse's station. Granddaddy walked over and Lily stood to hug him.

"She's all right, Lily. Mean as ever."

"Thank you, Jesus."

"Help me off this couch, old man." Millard reached out to Granddaddy.

We looked up as Grandma emerged, and she shot us a look that declared, "No more fuss." The nurse came over to her with a wheelchair.

"Really?" Grandma raised her eyebrows sky-high and nodded at the chair.

"Really," said the nurse. "Protocol."

"I don't mean this ugly, but your protocol should be reserved for actual patients, not folks who drop by for an hour to be poked, prodded and humiliated."

The nurse smiled at us. It was clear as the crystals around my neck that Ellen Robinson would be ordering the world to her satisfaction as usual.

"Be nice, Ellie," Granddaddy said.

"This is me being nice, Tom. You push me out of here now."

"With pleasure, my darling."

We made our way to the circular drive-up, where Daddy was waiting with the car. Grandma and Granddaddy settled in back together, hand in hand.

When we got back to Mama D.'s most of the visitors had gone. Sarah Anne was sitting in the living room waiting for us.

"Everything all right?" She glanced nervously at Grandma.

"It was a wasted trip, Sarah Anne. I told him," Grandma waved her hand in Granddaddy's direction, "but he wouldn't listen."

"Delaney, a boy left this for you," Sarah Anne handed me an envelope. It was a sympathy card in blues and greens with a glittery mountain scene on front. Maybe that was supposed to look like Heaven. When I opened it, I found: "You are in our thoughts and prayers." It was signed by every member of the First Baptist Youth Group, and Chris's signature was the tiniest of all, scrawled at the very bottom. I tucked it into my purse to place with the tear bottle and blue necklace deep inside my dresser.

That night I dreamed I was near an old church or castle with Mama D. She could walk and talk with me, and looked fine . . . but somehow I knew she was very fragile and had to leave me soon. She told me, "I will always love you, Delaney. Watch over your Daddy for me and take special care of him. He will need you now more than ever." When I looked up to answer, I was standing alone in a wide green field surrounded by low stone walls. Mama D. was gone.

Trouble, Part One

Delaney

Three weeks later I was sitting in the kitchen with my mom, having our hundredth argument of the morning.

"I don't need a babysitter. This is stupid. I'm almost twelve. I'm old enough to be *hired* as a babysitter, Mom."

"Delaney, that's true," she replied as she shoved a pan into the dishwasher. "But your dad and I are going to be gone two days, and you're not staying here alone. Jami has the flu and Hanna has an out of town game, so you can't stay with either of them. You'll have fun with Caitlin."

No, I wouldn't. "Mom, she is a complete bitch to me . . ."

"Language, Delaney."

"She may be over twenty now, Mom, but she's not as mature as I am. She will have her so-called fiance over here. I wouldn't be surprised if she decided to throw a naked pool party."

"That's not going to happen. Go get dressed for school. You're going to be late."

"Mom, I don't see why y'all have to go now, anyway. Can't you reschedule for next week? At least I could stay with a friend and not the Spawn of Satan."

"Enough, Delaney. Be downstairs in fifteen minutes or else." She threw the plates in like sideways frisbees, a sure sign I had better cooperate. I took the steps two at a time. My cousin Caitlin now insisted her name was "Caty." She had a nose piercing featuring a diamond booger and a tat on her hip the size of her foot, though Mom and Dad didn't know. It was Japanese for "You never step in the same river twice." Or maybe for "This girl is a bitch on wheels and I'm going to ink it on her because she will never know the difference." Whatever. If I was going to be stuck with her for two whole days—and one very long night—I would just have to deal. If creepy Duane came over, though, I would be locking myself in my room. I threw the closet door back, trying to decide what would express today's mood. Black. Yep, I would go with black head-to-toe. It would aggravate Mom and I would look skinny if I sucked in my stomach.

When I opened the front door she was already in the car, gazing out the side window at nothing. Dad had left the house really early. I heard him about five o'clock and rolled over to go back to sleep.

I threw my backpack on the floor and grabbed the seat belt. When I glanced at Mom I saw a wet track on her cheek. "Oh my God, Mom, what's wrong? Was it me? I am so sorry. I can't stand Caitlin, and you know it, but I can put up with her for a while. Mom. Mommy? Why are you crying?" I reached for her arm. "I am sorry," I repeated. "Please tell me what's going on."

"Nothing, Delaney. I am a little sad this morning. It's no big deal. I'm fine." She started the car and glanced in the rear view mirror, wiping her face with her pinkie fingertip.

I wasn't convinced, especially when she didn't bother to

comment on my outfit. Ordinarily, she would tell me I looked "Goth," whatever that was. Or ask if it would kill me to wear a brighter color, or at least nicer shoes. Mom was pretty good at playing fashion critic. If she didn't care today, she must really be upset. Neither of us said a word all the way to school. When we got in the drop-off line I told her, "I'll jump out at the end so you won't have to wait." I reached for the door handle.

"Delaney, don't worry. Everything is fine." She smiled the fakest smile ever and leaned over to kiss my cheek. "Have a great day, honey. You look beautiful."

That did it. Now I knew something was very wrong. "Mom, are you sure? We can always have a hooky day today. You could call me in sick and we could get lunch and shop or something."

"No, baby. I'll see you at three o'clock." She put the blinker on and got ready to fight her way out of line. "I love you, Delaney."

"I love you too." My stomach was somewhere slightly north of my knees. There was no way this day was going to be good at all. When I thought about it, there had been lots of whispered conversation around the house lately. Somewhere between losing Mama D., history homework, playing with Beastie and trying to keep my face from getting zits, I had missed something. *What was going on?*

"Delaney?" Kristin Herman was staring at me from the edge of her locker door, one eyebrow in the air. "Are you okay? You look a little sick."

"No, I'm fine. Just thinking."

"Well, if you don't stop thinking and grab your stuff you're going to be late for Blabby Abby."

Miss Abby Ferguson was our English teacher. She tended to drone in a monotone for thirty minutes without pausing for breath.

"Thanks."

She winked and tossed her long blond hair as she hurried off to join her boyfriend Todd. Everyone in my class had someone but me. Maybe today I would look thin enough . . .

"Miss Robinson?"

I managed to drop everything I was trying to take out of my locker at the assistant principal's feet, taking out her big toe with my five-pound Biology book.

"I'm sorry, Mrs. Dryden." I hurried to pick them up, trying to remember if last night's homework was in my green folder or blue one.

"Delaney, I need to see you in my office. Please come with me."

What had I done?

"Yes, ma'am." I followed her clicking heels, staring at the worn wood floor and mentally recounting my recent School Sins.

When I sat on her nasty green nubby couch—widely regarded as the closest thing to Hell at Folsom Middle School—Mrs. Dryden clasped her blue-veined hands on the desk and began, "Delaney, yesterday a student reported to me that you cheated on a Biology exam last week by copying your neighbor's answers."

"I don't know what to say, Mrs. Dryden, except that is ridiculous. I have never cheated. I don't need to." *I made a 92 on that test. I did not look away from my desk. What the . . .?*

"This is serious, Delaney. I am going to have to call your parents for a conference." She looked into my eyes, as though trying to gauge my poker face.

"That's fine, Mrs. Dryden. My mom should be home any time now."

Mrs. Dryface nudged her red reading glasses up her nose and glanced at my student records. She punched in our phone number, each long bleep stinging my ears. She stared at me as we listened to the loud ringing together. After eight rings, she hung up and announced, "I'll try to get this resolved as soon as possible. The student who says you copied their paper will be present as well. You may head to class now," she said, handing me a yellow pass, "and I would appreciate it if you would not discuss this with any fellow students."

"I won't, Mrs. Dryden." I gathered my dignity and headed for her door. "Mrs. Dryden?"

"Yes, Delaney?"

"If it was Rochelle Cochran, she hates me for a bunch of reasons. But I did not copy her."

"Just get to First Period, Miss Robinson."

"Yes, ma'am."

My mom always went straight home after dropping me off, to clean up the kitchen and fix her face. *Where was she?*

There is a big book of quotations on our living room table. I remembered one by Dorothy Parker, "What fresh hell is this?" I had no way of knowing at the time, but I was going to find out what she meant in a few hours.

"Welcome, Miss Robinson." Miss Ferguson snatched the pass from my hand and studied it for what seemed like five minutes. I heard the usual giggles from the back of the room and hurried to my desk.

Blabby Abby turned back to the screen she'd been pointing to when I arrived. "Who can tell me the author of this poem?" She scanned the room, crossing her arms. We had about one minute until she'd start tapping her toe. I read the words and tried to remember who wrote "Daybreak in Alabama."

"Come on, people. We talked about this yesterday." Her impatience was legendary, and I hoped someone would raise a hand soon. Terry Lovell shyly waved his fingers in the air.

"Terry?"

"Langston Hughes?"

"Excellent. That is correct. We are going to continue our study of Alabama poetry by writing some of our own." She picked up her trademark pink chalk and walked to the blackboard. "Let's start by listing all the things you can think of in our home state."

Everyone sat stock still. Once more, Terry's hand shot up. I was beginning to hate him.

"Red clay?"

She nodded and put it on the board. "More."

I raised my hand. "Pine needles with raindrops on them."
"Nice, Delaney."

Kristin offered, "Front porches and hugs." The whole class yelled out their thoughts as Blabby Abby scribbled furiously. "Cows in a pasture with fog, chickens, cotton fields, mountains, waterfalls, sweet tea, (the inevitable) blue skies . . ."

At that moment Miss Ferguson's speaker announced, "School will be closing in thirty minutes due to inclement weather in the vicinity. Bus riders should report to their areas in fifteen minutes. Car riders, contact your parents. You may come to the office to use the telephone if necessary."

If you live in Alabama, tornado warnings are a part of life. This was our equivalent of a snow day, and we were very happy about it. Books were gathered and poetry was avoided for a while longer. At least, that is what we thought.

"Class, I expect fifteen written answers to my question tomorrow," Miss Ferguson demanded. "Once you are safely home, do not forget."

We heard her, but were busy laughing and packing up.

Trouble, Part II

Lisa

Aaron. Benjamin. Ben Robinson? Caleb. Colin.

I love the name Colin because of an old boyfriend. My first real kiss was stolen in a dark school hallway in ninth grade, with Colin's beautiful lips tentatively brushing mine as he gathered my waist and pulled me closer, like something in a movie. He had the most amazing hands, with long slender fingers that were made for piano playing. Colin could make handing me a fork a sensual experience. He knew how to brush a girl's hair back and grip it at the nape of her neck for a kiss. I remembered him stroking my eyebrow softly with his thumb one time as I fell asleep with my head on his shoulder.

He broke up with me with no explanation one week before senior prom. My replacement date was my cousin Dean, four inches too short and plagued by allergies and remarkable acne. We agreed on a simple black tux to go with my red dress. My plan was to drive Colin wild with jealousy, staying as far away from my cousin as possible and dancing with selected members of the football team.

Dean showed up in a powder blue ensemble, handing over a yellow corsage and informing me, "I don't know how to dance, Lisa. My mom should not have told Aunt Ann this was a good idea."

We spent the evening sitting near the refreshments table. No one approached me for anything, except a girl from another school. She wanted to locate the restroom.

Colin didn't come to the prom.

I sighed and closed my eyes, slouching down in the plush pink chair and tracing "worst night ever" with my fingernail on the back cover of the baby name book. I was grateful there were only two other women sitting across the waiting room, both absorbed in Dr. Anderson's magazine collection.

Our most recent Christmas card from Colin featured a photo of him with his life partner Brad, each holding the hand of their adopted Chinese daughter Maya. My handsome dark-haired Colin had somehow morphed into Angelina Jolie.

"Lisa Robinson?" I jumped up and resisted the urge to raise my hand and say, "here." The nurse swung the office door open wide with her right arm and nodded me ahead. "So, how are we feeling today?"

Terrified and nauseated. "Fine," I answered. She led me to a cubicle that reeked of rubbing alcohol and pointed to a plastic chair with a fake wood desktop, then reached for my right wrist to tug my arm. The blood pressure cuff squeezed until I wanted to cry. I listened to the mechanical inflation and tried to remain serene.

"Do you still have periods, Mrs. Robinson?"

Well, that was insulting as hell. I was forty, not sixty. "Yes." I sneaked a look at my bp numbers, desperately searching for inner calm in the face of her question.

"When was the first day of your last period?" She frowned as she removed the cuff, then reached for a plastic stylus as she noted my chart. I sensed that I was boring her to death. I looked at the mint green wall as she attacked my index finger and drew blood.

"About six weeks ago. That's why I'm here."

She gave me a practiced smile. "Are you currently using any birth control?"

"No. I thought . . . well, my daughter is almost twelve, and we gave up on conceiving another baby years ago."

"So you think you may be pregnant?"

"Well, either that or something is wrong. I did a home pregnancy test and it was positive." I returned her smile, though mine was a little trembly.

"Let's see how much you weigh. Do you want to take your shoes off?"

Yes, I want to take my shoes off, and every other thing on my body weighing more than one ounce. "No, I'll keep them on. Please don't tell me what I weigh. I really don't want to know."

She chuckled—all one hundred former-cheerleader pounds of her—and began sliding the weights back and forth. I squeezed my eyes tightly shut and waited. She kept rearranging the scale, and I felt sure she was prolonging my agony for her amusement.

"Aww, that's not so bad." She offered me another tight smile—I noticed lipstick on one of her front teeth—and handed me a plastic cup. "First door on your left. Place the cup on the shelf when you're finished."

I clutched the Dixie Cup of Fate in my fist and wondered how I could handle all of this. Delaney was practically a young woman. Tommy had all sorts of plans for family travel. What if the baby had . . . problems? What if I miscarried? Should I tell my daughter what was going on? This was silly. Of course I was not pregnant. It was a fluke. My system was getting a bit erratic. No way I was pregnant. The nausea was just nerves.

By the time I was settled with the paper gown and lap cover in the freezing exam room, I was taking very deep breaths and wishing I were anywhere but there. The wall charts showing fetal development mocked me. The stirrups scared me as much as if I were about to board a Brahma bull. I cannot imagine a woman who does not hate gynecological exams. I wanted to run. I wanted to cry. I wanted to . . .

Knock-knock. "Lisa, you ready?"

"Yes," I called.

Dr. Anderson breezed into the room, her blond hair a fuzzy halo. She was five feet tall and mostly lab coat. "How are you feeling?" she asked as she washed her hands.

"Sick. Scared. Sick."

She scooted her stool closer to the exam table and patted my arm. "Does Tommy know?"

I don't even know. "No, I haven't said a word to anyone. Wait a minute. Are you saying I am pregnant?"

"You are a little over a month along." She smiled and pointed, "Feet there. Scoot down. You know how it's done."

Her nurse walked in, an older woman of about two hundred pounds with a sweet smile. "Hello, Mrs. Robinson."

I glanced at her name tag. "Hi, Delia."

She stood at my shoulder and gave it a reassuring squeeze. The ceiling had a mural of cherubic babies I'd not noticed before. By the time Dr. Anderson finished torturing me, I was dizzy with a fresh wave of nausea.

"Lisa, everything looks good. I'll wait for you in my office." Dr. Anderson nodded at my pile of clothes on the chair and offered me her brightest sunbeam of optimism look. "You're going to be fine. There are a few considerations based on your age, but there is every reason to believe you're going to have a happy, healthy baby in about eight months." She handed my chart to Delia, who pressed a green wall button to indicate they were moving on.

I desperately needed a saltine cracker, a therapist and my mother. In that order. When I had my clothes on I planted myself on the plastic chair and let a few tears fall, wondering how much longer the jeans would fit.

Dr. Anderson's office was decorated in deep blues and greens. Each book shelf featured small photos of the babies she'd delivered. Delaney was usually somewhere on my upper left, but I couldn't spot her. I settled into the armchair facing her desk and waited for her to begin. After two full minutes of reading my chart, she looked up.

"Lisa, I would recommend chorionic villus sampling when you're a bit further along, because there is some risk of chromosomal abnormality after the age of forty. It can be done much earlier in pregnancy than amniocentesis—at twelve weeks—so I think CVS might be your best choice. We do it here in the office. I am giving you a prescription for prenatal vitamins. Your blood pressure is a bit elevated, so we will need to monitor it closely. I want to see you every three weeks."

"Okay."

She scanned my face carefully. "Lisa, there is no reason to worry. Women your age carry healthy babies to term all the time."

"To be honest, that is only one of my worries, Dr. Anderson. I am in good shape, and I'll take care of myself. I'm more concerned at this point about the impact a baby is going to have on my family. Delaney has been the center of the universe for almost twelve years. My husband is semi-retired and planning all sorts of vacations for us. He has been researching a trip to Ireland. We were going to go early next year."

"Well, that is a trip you may want to postpone. You're due near the end of December." She walked around to my chair. "Everything is going to be fine," she patted my shoulder lightly, "and your husband will no doubt be thrilled when he hears the news. It will take Delaney a little longer, maybe, but she will be, too."

"If you say so." I stood to leave. "Dr. Anderson, how many women have second babies at my age? Do you see this a lot?"

"No. But I love it when I do." She grinned at me. "Be strong, woman."

"I don't have any other choice."

"Don't forget to schedule your next appointment on the way out." With that, she shrugged on her lab coat to move on to the next womb.

As I stepped outside I noticed the sky looked ominous. My cell phone rang and Delaney's voice announced, "Mom? School is closing early. I need you to pick me up right now."

There were at least fifty cars in the pick-up line ahead of mine. I noticed Helene Carlson standing next to her Range Rover, ear pressed to an iPhone and no doubt trying to coerce a banker into financing her latest real estate deal. She waved merrily at me, slipping her Ray Bans down a bit to be sure I saw her big blue eyes. *Yes, you look pretty Helene.* I drummed my fingers on the steering wheel. "Baby Come Back" came on the oldies station and I smashed the radio button in disgust. Delaney jerked the car door open and threw her backpack into the rear seat.

"Have you heard anything about the weather, Mom? Did you talk to Daddy?"

Delaney used "Daddy" when she was feeling nervous. Any other time it was "Dad" or "Father" when she was remonstrating him about something.

"No, I haven't. Let's get home and turn on the TV."

"Where were you this morning?"

"I had a doctor's appointment."

"Are you okay?"

"Yes, baby, I'm fine."

We noticed the wind picking up as we made our way through the heavy traffic. The grocery store parking lot was jam-packed with cars, a sign of the usual rush to batteries and bottled water.

Our local television station was wasting no time. "Cullman, Logan, Berlin . . . you should already be in your safe place. Do not attempt travel at this point. If you are in a car, take shelter under an overpass or in a ditch. This storm is headed your way and will arrive in less than five minutes." The local meteorologist was tugging his suspenders and turning to a map. "Winds of up to . . . what was that, Jim?" He paused. "We are receiving early reports of damage in the Tuscaloosa area. Folks, this is a monster tornado. I'm thinking an EF-4 or possibly even 5."

"Mom, is it coming here?"

"I don't know. I'm going to call your dad."

Tommy's cell phone rang and rang. I decided against leaving a panicky voice mail and hoped he was headed home.

"Delaney, find Beastie and go to the basement. I'll be down in a minute. We'll turn the TV on there."

"Where is Daddy?" she demanded.

"I don't know. Hurry up." Rain was hammering the roof. I watched a tree branch the size of my leg flying toward our neighbor's front window. Tommy's car was rounding the corner. I sighed with relief.

"Where is Delaney?" he asked, deadbolting the door. I wondered if that would do anything whatsoever to deter a tornado, but kept the thought to myself.

"She and Beastie are in the basement."

"Good. You get down there, too. I'll see you in a minute."

"Tommy, just forget the house and come on. Now."

"I'll be there soon, Lisa. Go." His eyes darted wildly around the room. I saw him running upstairs as I closed the basement door behind me. He must be heading for the safe in our closet, I thought. *Please God, keep us out of danger.* I looked down and noticed I was clutching my lower belly.

Delaney noticed, too. "Mom, are you feeling all right? It will be okay. Don't worry." She was curled up on the couch with Beastie in her lap. My protective eleven-year-old-going-on-twenty-five daughter.

"Fine, baby."

Sirens wailed in the distance. The dog buried his head under

Delaney's thigh as Tommy started down the stairs.

My husband's hair looked like a post-hurricane Florida palm. He still wore rain-soaked clothes from work, and his forced calm was betrayed by worried eyes. Tommy looked like he'd been on the roof checking the stability of shingles—something not entirely out of character for him, even in the face of imminent tornadoes. His cell phone was pressed to an ear, and he pinched the bridge of his nose. I heard him reassuring Ellen, promising to call and report in the wake of the storm. Then he joined us to watch disaster unfold on television.

Secrets

Tommy

I closed the bedroom door and then the bathroom door as quietly as possible.

"Are you home? I've been calling and calling."

"Yes, I just got here. The storms aren't even coming this way. Are *you* home?"

"Yeah. Lisa and Delaney are in the basement. I'm going down there, but I had to talk to you first."

"Well, I am flattered, Tommy. You haven't told her yet, have you?"

"Kara. It's not the right time. But I will. I *will*. I love you."

"I have to go. Be safe. I can't do this much longer, Tommy." She sighed deeply, and I could imagine her pacing between her kitchen and bedroom. "I am on the verge of being someone you used to know."

She was gone. I made my way to the basement and dialed my parents' number. "Mom? Are y'all in the hallway?"

"Yes, Tommy. We are hunkered down. This won't amount to anything here. I am worried about y'all, though. They say Tuscaloosa was hit hard, and it's coming your way."

"We will be fine, Mom. I'll call you when it's over." I spoke the last words as I jumped off the bottom step. Lisa and Delaney were glued to the television.

"Anything new?"

Lisa said, "Spann is saying that we should be all right, but Tommy, it's awful. They've been showing pictures from Tuscaloosa and Cullman. It looks like they're wiped out."

Delaney tossed the dog off her lap and crossed to the mini-fridge. "Daddy, do you want a Coke?"

"No thank you." I glanced at Lisa. As usual, she was combing her hair through her fingers and trying to find her reflection somewhere. I thought about Kara and her long tan legs. I thought about Memphis. I thought about her breath on my neck and her nails on my back.

"Daddy? I have a Snickers if you're hungry."

"No thanks, Delaney Doodle." My daughter was breaking my heart. *I* was breaking my heart. I wondered when I could tell Lisa about Kara. I tried to imagine if Delaney would ever speak to me again.

"Tommy?" Lisa was looking at me in the strangest way. Her head was cocked to one side.

"Yeah."

"Did you take the stuff out of the safe upstairs or leave it there?"

It took me a few beats to catch up. "No. I left it. Seemed best since we're in the clear." *Like I had known that.*

Two years ago I was sitting in the lobby of The Peabody in Memphis with some aviation industry execs. It was a typical convention—we were on our third round of afternoon drinks and waiting for the duck parade. I was bored and wishing I were home.

Wayne Sewell announced, "Me and my brother-in-law are planning to do a little shootin' at a pistol range in an hour or so. You gonna come along, Tommy Boy?" He tugged at the waistline of his jeans as he stood, attempting to cover a burgeoning beer belly. He had lived in Chicago for most of his life. Memphis was where he'd grown up, and he loved showing it off when we visited.

Wayne's business represented somewhere in the neighborhood of half a million dollars per year to my company. If he was in the mood for target practice, I was required to be. I thought I could handle myself respectably.

Guns and alcohol are a a Southern male tradition, and a trip to the shooting range seemed more manly than viewing prissy waterfowl. "I'll meet y'all back here in an hour," I said, tossing a fifty on the table for our server. We had put him through a lot since one o'clock. Wayne had started calling him "Little Elvis" after his second bourbon.

It was hard to miss the woman in the first stall. Her cowboy boots were covered in pink and blue flowers, and my eyes traveled up six miles of leg to the cutest butt I'd ever seen. Her tee shirt was black and low-cut. She didn't have a trace of make-up under those plastic safety goggles but her cheekbones cried, "model." Maybe "supermodel." Her long brown hair was in a ponytail. I watched as she raised the Luger revolver, expecting a less than spectacular performance. She squeezed off six shots. Three were dead on the red heart, two were center forehead, one was upper abdomen.

Wayne saw me looking at her and shook his head "no." I directed my attention to the pistol he'd handed me, a semi-automatic Glock 9mm. My first two shots missed the target entirely.

"Distracted, Tommy?" he grinned. "Her name is Kara Evans."

"You know her?"

"Kara's dad owns this place. She fills in occasionally behind the counter if someone calls in sick. When I met her she was a junior in high school. Sure has grown up nice." He leered Kara's way until she lowered her gun. She took a cloth from her pocket and wiped it clean, then walked outside.

"Well, it's none of my business, Wayne." I turned back to my target and squinted. The next shot would have removed hair if the silhouette had a beehive.

After thoroughly embarrassing myself in front of Wayne and Edmund, I stepped out the back door and dialed my home number.

"Hello?" Lisa sounded annoyed.

"Hey. Everything okay there?"

"Oh, it's lovely, Tommy. The dog vomited on the living room rug and I have to get Delaney to dance practice in twenty minutes. My life is rich and full. Hope you're enjoying your convention."

I may be a simple man, but I know sarcasm and a verbal storm brewing when I hear them.   "Sorry, honey. I'll be back Tuesday night."

"Okay. I have to run. Love you. Bye."

I wondered what happened to the marriage we'd had for the first ten years. Our conversational highlights had deteriorated to housework, Delaney's schedule, Lisa's hair appointments and the weather.

Wayne was talking to Kara when I returned, turning his gun back and forth for her to admire. He waved me over. "Kara, this is Tommy Robinson from Alabama. He's in the computer software business. Can't shoot worth a damn."

She extended the prettiest hand I'd shaken in forty years. "Nice to meet you. I work in software, too. I'm an engineer in Huntsville, and I've heard of Aviation Systems. Quite the Alabama success story, Mr. Robinson."

That was a pleasant surprise. "Thank you." I ventured a guess. "You work for Boeing?"

"Yes. I started with them right out of college." She glanced at the customers lining up at the counter. "Harry?" she called.

Harry shuffled out from behind a faded black curtain and grimly produced a stack of paper targets.

"It was a pleasure, gentlemen. I have to get on the road home. Early morning tomorrow." She flashed a row of perfect white teeth. "Hope to see y'all again."

By the time we got back to the hotel it was time for supper. Wayne insisted on taking me to a rib place on Beale Street. We drank too much and walked to the Peabody at midnight, surrounded by tiny white lights in the trees. There was no mention of anything other than his company's annual contract negotiation and Memphis music history. I was disappointed. I wanted to ask about Kara, but stopped myself five times.

"Good night, and thanks for a great time, Wayne." I started to exit the elevator and felt a firm hand on my shoulder.

"She wanted me to give you this. Said if you'd like to hire the brightest mind in the South, you should give her a call." The business card was formal. "Kara Lee Evans, Senior Software Engineer, The Boeing Company."

I effected nonchalance and tucked it into my pocket. "See you in the morning."

"Sleep tight, Tommy Boy." He grinned and backed toward his room down the hall.

I did not call Kara until my best employee abruptly left for Silicon Valley. Six months after we met in Memphis she was in my office for an interview, dressed in a white shirt and tight blue knee-length skirt. Her stiletto heels made her exactly my height.

The interview was a formality. I'd received her resume via email and would have offered any job in the place but mine. Thirty-two years old, Phi Beta Kappa at Sewanee, Summa Cum Laude at Vanderbilt, a meteoric rise at Boeing. I could not understand why she wanted to relocate, but wasn't about to ask. I said, "Welcome to Aviation Systems, Miss Evans. When can you start?"

"In two weeks. My boyfriend is moving to Atlanta, and I have to help."

Ah. Boyfriend. Moving closer to the boyfriend. Of course.

"Your desk awaits, Kara. We will be happy to have you." I stood to shake her hand.

"One more thing," she replied, "I want close personal instruction from you." She gave me her sexiest smile and gathered her purse off the floor, a long fringed suede thing. "Is it all right if I call you Tommy?"

"Sure. We are very informal around here."

"Tommy, I have been watching your company for a long time and waiting for an IPO. Is that going to happen?"

Another piece of the puzzle.

"No. I have no plans right now, at least."

"Scott manages a hedge fund."

"Does he, now?" *Scott, The Boyfriend, I presumed.*

"He says you would make a killing."

I shuffled some papers around and wondered if I were making a mistake in hiring her. "I'll see you in two weeks, Kara."

She developed a new program within four months to increase our profitability by fifteen per cent. We booked presentations in Chicago (Wayne was very happy to see us) and Los Angeles. The two of us became friends and she mentioned inviting Lisa and me to her wedding in July. When Scott got cold feet and left her for another woman, guess where she turned for comfort?

"Tommy? You look like you're a million miles away." Lisa was scratching my head with her fingernails.

"No, I'm listening to the TV. We can go up now and look around. I suspect we have some roof damage." My cell phone rang, and Lisa's did, too. The calls from everyone we knew were starting. After assuring friends and relatives we were okay, we started our own series of calls to check on the ones we worried about. Alabama had been ravaged.

We Are Not in Kansas Anymore

Abby Ferguson

April 27th was just another day. I would spend seven hours trying to spark some appreciation for literature in restless and bored sixth and seventh graders. I would eat my Subway sandwich in the faculty lounge, hoping that Luke Bradley would walk in and notice my new haircut. I would ride my bike home and my roommate Becca and I would probably order pizza and argue about television channels. I would get to sleep early, because teachers rise with the dawn. Daybreak in Alabama fetched this Shawnee, Kansas girl every morning.

I had grown to love the state after following Becca to the University of Alabama six years ago. We were lucky to find jobs in the same town after graduation, though she was increasingly unhappy with the bank and its politics. Folsom Middle School had its own peculiar politics, but I was happy in the classroom and had no intention of returning to Kansas. Mom and Dad did not understand at all. They visited a lot when the Crimson Tide was playing, but Alabama football was apparently the only thing that would entice them. I hadn't seen them since I took off the cap and gown and we feasted on barbecue at Tuscaloosa's legendary Dreamland, Dad with sauce all over his white shirt.

The early school dismissal was no surprise. Our favorite weatherman, James Spann, had informed us yesterday that strong storms were possible. I watched my first period class pack up and reminded them to be safe and smart. Then I proceeded to do the exact opposite.

No one wants to ride a bike in the pouring rain. I decided to settle in and grade some papers. My room was in an interior part of the building and I am, after all, from Kansas. Tornado sirens there inspire panic—here, they are a mere annoyance. The last thing I remembered for months was that Lizzie McDonald had finally learned the difference between an adjective and an adverb.

I heard people calling my name but could not answer. I tried to scream and found that there was no sound left in me. Something was holding my legs down, and I could feel water dripping on my face. Later I would discover it was mixed with lots of blood, and that is why I had trouble seeing in the dim light. I heard thunder, and I could make out the shape of a tree in the corner where my file cabinet once stood.

The doctors told me I laid there for three hours before the rescue team was able to dig me out. I owe my life to a dog named Sparta. She led the EMS workers to my battered body.

"Battered" hardly seemed sufficient to me. In addition to multiple leg fractures and a collapsed lung, my forehead was torn apart. They thought it was the tree. One of my biggest worries was whether I'd have a functioning left eye. Becca would not offer me a mirror, though it had been seven days since the storms. She cooed, "You are going to be fine, Abby. It's going to take time." My Mom

and Dad said the same thing. I saw the fear in their eyes and
wondered if "fine" would ever be possible.

Our principal, Faith Gorey, delivered a huge card signed by my
students. She placed a hand on top of mine. "Most of the school's
roof was blown off, and damage is estimated at about two million
dollars. Classes are suspended until the school board figures
something out." She paused and swept the hair out of her eyes,
glancing at the monitor by my bed. "No one else has been found in
the building, Abby. William wasn't there, but he wasn't home, either.
No one knows . . ." She shook her head.

William was a nice man of about fifty or so. He was the head of
our maintenance department and had six children.

"What were you thinking, Abby? We could have lost you." Now
she was crying. "Luke's house is completely leveled. It was directly
in the tornado's path. He was in a church shelter, and has gone to
stay with his family in Heflin. He says he will look for a place to
rent when school starts back." She forced a cheerful expression and
patted my hand. Apparently, my crush on Luke was more public
that I'd thought.

"What are the doctors telling you?" she asked, though I had a
feeling she knew more than I did. Faith didn't miss much.

"My legs will work again after physical therapy. They took the
ventilator away yesterday since I can breathe okay now. The part
they don't mention is my face. No one says much about my face,
Faith." I regarded her with my right eye. The left was still covered
with gauze.

She gazed at her lap. "Honey, you will be as beautiful as ever
when those bandages come off. Stop worrying about it."

My hand wandered reflexively to the clotted area above the
wrappings. I had already discovered my baldness, though I still had
long hair on each side. Mom brushed it gently every day.

Faith jumped up and grabbed the card from the room's only
table. There were several flower arrangements beside it. I could not
remember who had sent them, other than the daisies my mother

always selected for hospital occupants.

"Lewis drew you on the front," she offered. Lewis Ledbetter was the most talented artist in seventh grade. My portrait had been executed in crayon and was surrounded by trees and birds. I basked under a brilliant, cloudless blue sky. I looked happy. They'd even drawn my cat, Oscar Wilde Thing, though none of them had met him. The likeness was obviously copied from the picture on my desk. She opened the card and read, "Miss Ferguson, we are thinking about you and praying for you. We miss you a lot. Get better soon. We love you."

Now I was crying, at least as well as I could manage with one eye. Faith replaced the card and turned to leave. "Abby, are your parents going to stay?"

"Trust me, they will be here at least until I get out of the hospital. Mom is in Emergency Mode."

"They are in the apartment with Becca?"

"That's right. Mom has probably disinfected the entire place and most of town by now." I realized I didn't know how much of town was left. "Is the mall still there? What else was destroyed?"

"We were lucky, Abby. Sixteen people lost their homes and a lot more were damaged, but the school took the hardest hit. Almost all our businesses were spared. The only reported local death was a little girl whose bedroom caved in under a tree. Moore's Dairy is missing five cows. They're just . . . gone. A boy named Chris Jackson is in the ICU upstairs, but he is expected to recover. We are still hoping to hear about William." She walked over and tugged the window curtains shut, then headed for the door. "I'll be back soon, honey," she called.

The smell of today's lunch delivery flooded the room as she entered the hall. *Chicken,* I thought. I was still eating via tube.

I shut my eye and let the painkillers float me away.

A Writer Is Unwound

Abby Ferguson

Becca and my mother were sitting by the bed when I woke to bright sunlight. Two weeks had passed, and they were joining me for the removal of my eye bandages. Becca called it "See Day."

"How do you feel, honey?" Mom had moved to hover near my head. I was sure she was as curious as I to see the damage.

"Like a Cyclops awaiting a miracle, Mom."

She issued her reassuring smile and stroked my side hair. I hated that because it reminded me the front was obliterated.

"Dr. Hector will be here soon. He had an emergency surgery."
I turned my eye to Becca. She was eating a bagel and offered me a bite. I was happily surprised to find I wanted it.

Dr. Hector and his nurse of the day—I thought this one was Cheryl—came in bearing a tray loaded with scary-looking instruments. After perfunctory greetings he sat at my side and began removing the layers.

"Keep it closed, Abby. Your left eye is going to have to adjust gradually." He nodded to Cheryl, who shuttered the blinds and curtains.

My vision had always been 20/20. I held my breath and waited for instructions as I felt the last of the bandages come off. Dr. Hector applied some sort of potion on my eyelid, stroking it softly. It seemed as though twenty minutes went by. I heard my mother move to the left side of the bed and imagined her nervously wringing her hands.

"Okay, Abby. You can open it now."

My instinct was to scream. There was nothing but black. I blinked a few times and found I could decipher shapes, although they were blurry and confusing. When I added my right eye, I could see Dr. Hector carefully replacing scissors on his tray. I closed it and tried using the left again. My room was a nightmarish mix of fuzzy blobs.

Cheryl handed him a small flashlight and he examined both eyes. I found myself squeezing the left one tightly shut.

"You'll need some time, Abby. Don't expect to see well with that one until tomorrow. I promise you, it will get much better." He stood and patted my shoulder. "You're a lucky girl."

Oh, yes. I feel very lucky.

"Thank you, Dr. Hector." I turned onto my right side and regarded the dark window with both eyes. The left itched and tears flowed from it, crossing the bridge of my nose into the right.

"Abby, I brought your laptop." Becca entered my view. "Seems like a good time to finish your short story. The competition is open for another month."

I had forgotten about the southern fiction contest. One of our neighbors was a retired librarian from Montgomery, and she'd told us an interesting tidbit from her childhood that inspired me to write. I'd started my entry a week before the tornado. It was finished, but I'd wanted to do revisions.

"I'll think about it, Becs. If the two of you don't mind, I'd like to get some sleep."

Mom and Becca gathered their things and obediently headed for the door after kissing the side of my head.

Becca called, "I'll be back tonight, Abby, to see what you've written. I'm cooking a chicken casserole for your folks. You will have plenty of time."

Lucky girl. I drifted off to sleep contemplating what part of this adventure qualified as "luck."

When I awoke, I flipped the switch for the fluorescent light over my bed and opened the laptop. After a minute or two, I found I could see well if I closed my left eye. *The Cycle* was on my desktop. I opened it and read.

"The twins had a thin stream of evil running through them and it grew wider with each passing year. A stranger might only have noted two exceptionally beautiful, identical blond blue-eyed girls with charming smiles. Their mother knew better from the start. Herb's Grandmother Ledbetter had warned her just after their wedding, handing over her sour admonition along with a jar of homemade pickles—twins run in the family, and they almost always portend bad things to come. At the time, Arlee had ignored the crazy old woman as she was not given to superstition.

She subscribed on January 28th, 1933. Something in her—call it woman's intuition—knew the truth immediately: her baby girls were different, somehow. They took no notice of her unless they were hungry or needed changing. She was merely incidental.

Corine's was an easy birth, but Arlee was gripped just afterward with violent contractions that folded her body in two. Dorine came through the birth canal as though scratching and tearing her way out, struggling to pull whatever goodness and decency she might from her mother's body.

Mrs. Greeson, the gray-headed midwife, said Arlee had lost a lot of blood. She needed bed rest for two weeks, and Herb was to summon her immediately if the heavy bleeding resumed. She had done what she could. She placed the tiny red babies, peacefully sleeping, on either side of their mother. Arlee awoke to their urgent cries. It didn't take long to discover the first truth of the twins: they could not bear to be more than a foot apart. When placed together, they would close their eyes and drift off, their dimpled arms touching. They were, and remained, singularly focused on their oneness.

There was another thing—both had port-wine stain birthmarks on their left buttocks. Corine's was a wee bit larger, but both shared an unmistakable shape. The twins were branded with a tiny heart, as if to make up for the one they seemed to miss in other ways.

Herb was enchanted by his baby girls, and petted them from the beginning. He took them to town, one in each arm. The people would tell him how beautiful they were, how lucky he and Arlee should feel. Only the ones old enough to remember Herb's great-grandfather and his twin brother stared in fascination and wondered if these girls were more of the same.

Corine and Dorine thought as one. There was never any of the twins' wanting to establish unique personae. They insisted on the same clothes, the same everything. If forced to wear different outfits, they were miserable. Later, Arlee would think: *if one has the beginning of a decent thought or urge, the other will take it and turn it into something dark.* It was true of both her daughters.

When they were four, Michael was born. Corine and Dorine were playing in the yard when he arrived at 3:47 p.m. on July 7th. Arlee showed them their baby brother and they exchanged giggling glances that made her heart tendril into her throat. Two days later, she found them placing pillows over Michael's face as he lay sleeping. They said he'd been crying, and the noise bothered them. Michael had been asleep on his pallet for hours. Arlee scolded the twins severely and took to keeping the baby at her side whenever possible. If left defenseless, Michael would invariably be found screaming, unable to articulate what caused the trickle of blood on his arm or later, the bruises on his head. His first word was "help."

It seemed to Arlee that the girls were inclined to leave their brother alone when he became able to tell on them. The reports grew less frequent, and Michael gave them a wide berth.

At five and nine, Arlee saw that her children had established a kind of peace. The girls kept to themselves, and Michael never spoke to them more than necessary. He had his friend Benjamin from down the road and the boys played well together. They built roads in the dirt out back, driving their wooden cars through them over and over. Corine and Dorine had playmates, too, but remained aloof and inseparable even in groups. Their teacher, Mrs. Donal, told Arlee, "They are excellent students. My only concern is their lack of social interaction. I figure twins must be that way, focused more on one another."

When the girls were ten years old, there was a fire in the one-room schoolhouse. It started mysteriously in the middle of the night, a night when Arlee looked into their rooms to find them missing. Panicked, she searched until she found them in the barn, huddled together and whispering. They told her they'd been frightened by a noise, and didn't want to wake their parents. They'd come out to investigate on their own.

Ten year old innocents.

School commenced in the Baptist church a mile away, a longer walk for the children. Arlee expected complaints, but she got none. She discovered later that the twins were stopping children, including Michael, at the bridge over a nearby creek. They would demand anything of value in exchange for immunity to their "set-ups." It was a system they'd devised to accuse and convict their schoolmates of various crimes. Corine and Dorine were model students; they were innocent of any misbehavior in their entire school careers. They made very credible "witnesses."

When Michael was twelve, all he wanted in the world was a shotgun to hunt with his father. Arlee and Herb tried to explain to him that such an extravagance was impossible; he'd have to make do with sharing his father's old gun for a few years. Times were hard, and Christmas gifts had been meager throughout the children's lives. This year would be no different. In fact, there would be almost nothing under the tree.

Michael persisted. He developed a sort of magical thinking, believing that somehow, some way, his gun would materialize. It was his only desire. He had been a good boy. He wanted to use it to hunt food for his family. Why wouldn't God let this little prayer of his come true?

All through November, he stared at the magazine photo he'd pasted to his bedroom wall—the Browning Superposed Over Under Shotgun. In December, he walked into town twice just to view it in a shop on Noble Street. Mr. Harris even let him touch it.

Christmas morning, the family gathered around the tree together, their ritual. No one was allowed near it until they'd all assembled downstairs.

Michael took one look and screamed with joy. Tucked behind a rectangular box was a gift wrapped in shiny red paper, unmistakably a shotgun. He ran to the tree and ripped it open, uncovering a gun crudely carved of wood, his sisters' handiwork. The girls smiled, their eyes following him as he ran from the room, crestfallen. Arlee was rendered speechless with anger. Herb, finally grasping what his wife had tried so hard to define for fifteen years, herded the twins to their room and ordered them to stay there until he decided their punishment. They weren't even fazed. Their smiles remained in place as they marched upstairs. They weren't bothering to pretend remorse these days.

Herb wanted them to stay home for the rest of Christmas vacation and keep them busy with chores all day. Arlee had a different idea—separate them for the first time in their lives. Corine could remain at home and Dorine could spend the next week and a half at Herb's mother's house five miles away. They could use their time helping at each place. It would do them good to be apart.

The girls never batted an eye when the news was delivered. Arlee and Herb, curiously unfulfilled, went to Michael's room next. They promised him they'd put the money together for the gun within the next year, in time for fall hunting season. Michael's tear-stained face broke their hearts. They handed him his present, a rectangular box with new shoes. There was also an orange and some vanilla taffy.

In two hours, they'd go to Memaw's house to celebrate Christmas. Herb would discuss it with his mother, but was sure Dorine's help would be very welcome.

Mary Carter would be happy to host her granddaughter, though Herb thought she seemed the slightest bit hesitant. He hugged his mother, thanking her and extracting a promise for days filled with work—hard, character-building work. His mother's farm presented plenty of opportunity. Since his daddy's death five years ago, there had been a series of hired hands. None stayed longer than a month or two. She couldn't afford to pay them.

The next morning, Corine was waiting at the kitchen table when Arlee came down to brew the coffee. Her long blond hair was up in a bun and she was dressed for work. Arlee was encouraged.

It wasn't Corine.

Dorine had walked home after gathering eggs before dawn, leaving her suitcase sitting by her bedside. She'd crept into her room, lying beside her sister and wrapping her arm around her sleeping back. When it began to get light outside, Corine headed to her grandmother's, taking Dorine's place in the barn. Somehow, they'd known when the time was right to switch back. No one ever knew they saw each other daily for the entire "separation."

Arlee and Herb saw the girls functioning apart and felt they'd done something very healthy for them. Corine and Dorine would now be required to contribute a portion of whatever money they could earn toward Michael's shotgun, the balance of their punishment. They took a job after school helping Mr. Peterson stock his drugstore shelves. They told him he could have two for the price of one, and he couldn't pass up the opportunity. The girls were pretty and hard-working. They gladly interrupted their work to help customers find what they needed. It was a real bargain.

Corine and Dorine were eventually promoted to run the cash register when Mr. Peterson was busy in the back. As Wayne Gibson slid his package of Trojans onto the counter, eying the ceiling anxiously, it was Dorine who took his $1.28. She grasped his right hand from underneath, slowly placing the change onto his palm with her left, blue eyes locked on his. The twins laughed as a clearly flustered Wayne fumbled the door closed, bells tinkling. They were sixteen, and had discovered a new game. There were lots of possibilities.

They took Dennis Mitchell into the storeroom, luring him with smiles and promises of stolen kisses from them both. Dennis, married and father to two, found himself surrendering twenty dollars in exchange for the photo Dorine took. Mr. Peterson had gone home sick. It was something he ate.

It was arsenic. Just a trace, hidden in his coffee. As the months unfolded, he found himself taking more and more trips to the doctor with vague complaints: nausea, headache, tingling in his fingers. The tests revealed nothing abnormal. He decided he was working too hard, and handed the store over most evenings to the twins. They were happy to help and he felt good with both of them there, especially on one meager salary.

By July, the girls had amassed more than enough money to buy Michael's longed-for Browning, but they kept that to themselves. It would be difficult to explain the various sources of income they'd developed through the drugstore. They'd let Michael and the rest of the family wait until October, when they'd cheerfully hand over twenty-five dollars for their brother's cause. Along with Arlee and Herb's savings, it was enough. Michael slept with the loaded gun under his bed. He decided he was old enough at thirteen to help defend against intruders in the unlikely event there ever were any. He felt like a man.

In November, Corine and Dorine made their first big mistake, trying to shake down James Wilton after photographing him with Corine sitting atop stacks of Coca Cola fountain syrup, his hand up her skirt. He told them they'd never get a damned penny from him, and demanded the film from the camera *Or Else*. They aimed their tinkling laughs at him and told him he'd never get his hands on the camera. It was safely hidden in their secret place. James made a terrible mess, tearing the storeroom apart. They had to work hard to hide it from Mr. Peterson. It was a close call, and gave the girls pause. They decided to re-think their scheme.

Just after midnight on the 24th, James Wilton slid open the window to the twins' room. He gently shook Dorine's shoulder, straining to see in the moonlight and clamp his hand over her mouth. He whispered to her, "Surrender the camera and film, and I'll be be on my way, bitch."

Corine's scream was louder than his ears could've imagined. Both Herb and Michael came running with baseball bats and a Browning Superposed Over Under Shotgun. When they swung the door open, Herb threw on the light and found a man he assumed was there to rape his daughters. He stepped forward with the bat, but Michael had already fired a haphazard shot.

He hit Dorine, killing her instantly.

By the time Sheriff Knowles arrived, Corine was covered in her sister's blood and sitting in the corner, catatonic. James Wilton was handcuffed and arrested for burglary and attempted rape. Michael was led away, too, amid his mother's screams and sobs.

Michael was acquitted of homicide, but James served six long years in prison. Corine never spoke another word, allowing herself to be led away to the county's mental health institution after three months of staring into space. She lived the rest of her sixty-two years there, never interacting meaningfully with another soul.

Michael gave his beloved shotgun to his old friend Benjamin—he could no longer bear those arms. At twenty-two, he married lovely eighteen-year-old Wendy Barnes. Their son Billy arrived in 1960.

Wendy struggled to get pregnant again after Billy's birth, and Michael found himself stroking her hair night after night, whispering, "It will be all right. We will have more children, I know it. God will bless us again, just as He has with our curly-haired little boy."

In 1977, Wendy and Michael packed their only son off to college and settled into life as a couple again. Arlee died in 1978; Herb had passed on years before, never recovering from the loss of his daughter.

1979 brought a miracle: Wendy was astounded and thrilled to discover that at thirty-nine, she was expecting a baby. Later came the news that she was going to bear twins. The sonogram showed two perfect little girls, their tiny arms intertwined, both sucking their thumbs.

Michael was equally thrilled, though less astounded. After all, twins ran in his family. He couldn't wait to meet his daughters. He started up the stairs, the jar of pickles Wendy craved constantly in his hand."

As I typed the final paragraph, Jenny came into the room. She was my favorite charge nurse, usually sporting scrubs covered in daisies.

"How do you feel?" she asked.

"Like a train wreck covered in touch-up paint."

"I see the language part of your brain is intact. Let's check your vitals."

After she noted my chart, she nodded at the laptop. "Are you working on something?"

"I finished it as you came in. It's a short story I'm thinking of entering in a contest."

"I didn't know you were a writer. My grandmother is a writer. Her name is Sarah Anne Robinson. She has articles in lots of magazines."

"I'm not. I'm a lowly English teacher, but like everyone in the world I fancy myself an author."

Jenny smiled and crossed to open the curtains. "I think you'll be leaving us soon. I'm going to remove the bandage on your forehead. You'll have lots of pretty sutures to look at."

"Are you aware that no one has let me hold a mirror? My mom and Becca are afraid I will lose it when I see the damage."

"That's ridiculous. You look great. When I'm done, I'll bring you a mirror and help you with a bit of fixing up if you'd like. Dr. Edwards will be here in an hour to see how your wound is healing, and you're scheduled for Ortho tomorrow. You're getting a new leg cast and crutches."

"Wow. I didn't realize you all were going to release me into the wild so soon."

"In two days, probably. We are getting tired of you." She winked and went to work on the tape holding my head together. "Feeling brave? I don't think this will hurt much. Or as we like to say, you may feel a little discomfort."

Jenny was gentle and I couldn't complain. The bandage had itched for days. The cast was driving me crazy, too. It would be a huge relief to get a new one.

She pressed the button to sit me as upright as possible and said, "I'll be right back. Prepare to smile at yourself."

"I cannot promise that."

"Then no mirror for you, missy."

"Okay, Jenny. Let me see the damage."

My first impression was *I have a permanent Frankenstein Line above my left eyebrow.*

"Will that go away?"

"It'll fade, but you will probably need surgery to fix it permanently. Dr. Edwards is really good. He will explain your options."

I sighed and asked, "Do you have some mascara and lip gloss?"

"Atta girl. I'll get my purse. You have to promise not to tell anyone I shared mascara with you, and you have to let me apply it. I have a new lip gloss. You can keep it."

"I love you, Jenny."

"Will you let me read your story while I'm at lunch?"

"Yes, ma'am."

"Deal." She took my computer and returned with cosmetics. Jenny was good at painting, and I was encouraged. There was nothing on television worth watching, so I closed my eyes to nap and try to grow my hair.

Dr. Edwards seemed pleased with my efforts at healing. "I want you to schedule an appointment with my office in six weeks, Abby. During that visit we will discuss follow-up options."

"You mean surgery? Laser treatments? What?"

"At this point, I would say surgery will be indicated. Let's wait and see."

"Will my insurance cover more surgery?" I asked.

He glanced at my chart. "Probably not, I'm afraid. For the time being, I want you to apply the ointment I gave you three times a day. In six weeks we will see where we are."

"Thank you, Doctor."

"My pleasure, Abby. Call my office tomorrow. Don't forget." He left a card on my bedside table and was gone.

Almost immediately, Jenny brought my laptop and plunked it on the bed. "Girl, you can write. You can write like a house on fire. I loved the story. Very Stephen King-ish."

"You really think so?"

"Yes I do. You should definitely enter the contest."

Damages

Ellen

I set the kitchen table for two and waited for Tom to get off the phone. After fifteen minutes I put the chicken salad and bread out. He could build his own sandwich. I sat down with my mixed greens and opened my favorite magazine.

"I am going to have to go down there in person. Damned insurance. You pay and pay and they're never there when you need them." Tom slapped his newspaper on the table and crossed to the counter. "How many years we been dealin' with Joe Meyers, Ellie? They can't even get an adjuster over here after two weeks?"

"Tom," I began, "we have had this discussion. The entire state was hit hard. I am sure the damage to the garage and your car is not at the top of their priority list. Many people lost their homes and everything in them."

"I know that, but there's been plenty of time for Joe to see about my situation. I am going over there this afternoon. That secretary of his is giving me the runaround. I was on hold forever, and then she told me he was gone to lunch. I did not just fall off the back of a turnip truck."

I rolled my eyes. "Don't shoot your mule, honey."

Tom's great uncle Weston had a legendary temper. One spring afternoon during the Depression his mule stopped in the middle of a field and refused to take another step. Weston responded by marching back to the house, retrieving his gun and promptly shooting the mule in the head. As the mule was his most valuable farm implement, it was safe to assume he regretted it. Family lore had evolved into a nice catchphrase for generations of women who married into the Robinson family.

Tom settled across from me with a huge sandwich and a pile of forbidden potato chips, shooting a defiant glance my way before covering his face with the paper. He shook it twice to widen the pages.

I returned to a peach cobbler recipe and waited for him to interrupt my reading. As I mentally checked off ingredients, he began reading the obituaries.

"Do we know a Simpson in Ohatchee?"

"I don't think so, Tom."

"Says here he was sixty-eight. Younger than me. I think I knew his brother."

"Maybe you did."

"What are you doing this afternoon?" He lowered the newspaper to see what I was trying to read. "You gonna make that?"

"No, I was just looking over the recipe. Or trying to." I took my empty salad bowl to the sink, praying he'd hush for a while.

"Looks like our GM stock is down again."

"Uh huh. I'm going out to work in the garden."

"It's too hot out there, Ellie."

"No, it's not. I'll wear a sunhat."

I closed the back door, wishing Annie were still alive. We had the sweetest cocker spaniel in the world, and she didn't ever bother me when I tried to read.

A few minutes later I saw him walk out to the garage for the hundredth time this week. His precious '66 Mustang lived in there and a pine tree had fallen on the roof during the storms. The damage to the car was minimal, but he acted like it was the end of the world. He'd patched the ceiling with our neighbor's help. Every day he paced around, waiting for the insurance company to respond to his demands for inspection.

"I'm going to give those people a piece of my mind." He had wandered over to his favorite chair under the oak tree. "Might take a little nap first."

"Okay, honey." I used my clean hand to tip my hat at him. "Want me to wake you up?"

"If you don't see me by three o'clock, yes. Are those geraniums or nasturtiums?"

I answered, "Geraniums, Tom." *The millionth time.*

He shoved his hands into his khaki shorts pockets and yawned. "I'll see you later, sweetheart. What are you cooking for supper?"

"Arsenic chicken."

"Sounds good."

"With hemlock potatoes."

"Guess I'll go lie down and work up an appetite."

"You do that. I'll get you up in time to attack the evil insurance empire."

"Thanks, Ellie. You're my best girl." He planted a sloppy kiss on my cheek, groaning as he stood. "Maybe I'll take you to McDonald's for supper."

"That would be lovely."

"Sounds safer for me."

"Sleep tight."

The garden was my haven, a place for precious silence and quiet thought. I could pull weeds for hours and enjoy it as long as the temperature didn't get too high and the bugs were at bay. I clipped ten of my prettiest Sonia roses after I finished working and walked to my leatherleaf fern patch. We would have a nice centerpiece in the dining room for Tommy and Lisa tomorrow night. They were dropping Delaney off for the weekend. Tommy had called yesterday and said, "Lisa and I need some time alone."

They'd canceled their trip to Atlanta when the tornadoes came through. I thought my son sounded stressed, probably because he worked too hard. I went to wake Tom from his nap, wishing Tommy would relax and enjoy his life more often.

Black Heart

Kara Lee Evans

I had some great places to shop in Memphis and Huntsville, but the choices near me now were frustrating. I wandered the lingerie department in our town's only decent store for thirty minutes trying to find an ensemble for my next visit from Tommy. The racks were full of frumpiness. I needed frisky.

"Do you have anything a little more sexy?" I asked the fat old saleslady, holding up a satin nightgown. "I have an important evening with my boyfriend."

She raised her head slowly from the checkout desk. I sensed her annoyance at my interrupting her secret candy bar break. "Did you see the black lace teddy on the mannequin? That's about the best we've got."

"I saw it, but was hoping for something a bit more unusual."

"I think Frederick's of Hollywood still has a catalog." She was smirking at me.

I turned my back on her rudeness and returned the gown to its rack. My cell started playing Tommy's song.

"Hey," he whispered.

"Hey yourself.," I answered.

"Where are you?"

"At the gym working out."

"Will you be back in the office soon?"

"I have to shower," I ran my fingers through my hair, "and get dressed. I'll be at my desk by two o'clock."

"Okay. Or you could take the afternoon off and meet me somewhere."

"Hannigan's?"

"I'll see you there at three. Park out back."

The man was an idiot. "Of course I'll park out back, Tommy. I'll cover my car with tree branches if you'd like."

"There is no need for sarcasm, Kara."

"There is no need to instruct me in discretion, Tommy." I smiled and hung up.

Hannigan's was predictably empty. I settled into a corner booth and ordered a Cosmo. Tommy arrived looking frazzled and slid in next to me.

"What's wrong?" I asked, stroking his hand.

"Lisa says she has something to discuss with me. I have no idea what that means, but she had me call my mom and arrange for Delaney to stay there this weekend."

"Do you think she knows?"

"Of course not, but I'm ready, Kara. I am going to tell her."

"It's about time. I am tired of this sneaking around shit, Tommy. You promised me you were going to leave her a month ago." I slid my skirt up to mid-thigh and placed his hand there.

"It's not that simple, Kara. You know that. My relationship with my daughter is the most important thing in the world to me." He paused and stroked my leg. "Delaney and you."

Nice recovery, Tommy.

"She'll forgive you. It will take time, but she will. I am looking forward to getting to know her."

He took his hand back to the table, patting it nervously. "Delaney is special, Kara. She is no ordinary eleven-year-old. Sometimes it seems like she was born grown-up. Very smart. Very precocious. Very judgmental. It will take her a long time to accept you."

I gathered my hair into a ponytail and sat up straight. "I'm good with kids."

"You're good with everything."

"Speaking of that . . . are you going to be with Lisa all weekend?"

"It depends on how things go. I have no idea how she'll react. She's been weird lately, keeping to herself and staying quiet. I don't know what's up with her. She keeps complaining that she's tired. Three days in a row she's been asleep on the couch when I got home. That is not like Lisa. She's always been in constant motion."

"Well, she's getting older. Probably just slowing down." I kissed his ear. "I don't mean that ugly."

He laughed halfheartedly. "Yes you do. She is only eight years older than you, Kara. My wife is still a beautiful woman. I'm sure she'll replace me in no time at all."

"I'm sure she will. This is best for all of us. You'll see."

"I wish I were as sure as you are. Kara, I'm not filing for divorce right away. I am going to tell Lisa about us. I am going to get my own place . . ."

"Why the hell not?"

"Because I need to get my head straight. There's a lot on the table. I need to think about money, and consider custody arrangements for my daughter. I can't neglect Aviation Systems. I'm worried about the effect this will have on my folks, too. They will not take it well. Actually, that is the understatement of the century.

My mom will go ballistic."

"I have ballistics experience." I put my hand over his and massaged his palm with my thumb. I knew that Tommy liked my way with a pistol. Most Southern men appreciated a woman who knew how to use a gun.

"Not funny. You haven't met Ellen." He pulled away and drummed his fingers. "Do you want another drink?"

"No."

"Want to ride to Birmingham with me? I'm free until seven."

"Yes."

I could tell by his expression what he planned in Birmingham. Tommy slapped a ten on the table and headed for the parking lot. As usual, I waited a full minute and followed.

I opened the driver's door of his car and moved the seat back. Tommy was pleasantly surprised as I climbed onto his lap, gripping his waist with my knees. We didn't get on the road until four thirty, but he did not mind at all.

The Weekend

Tommy

The landscape lights around the pool shined softly, casting a golden glow on my wife's face. She still looked every bit the blond beauty queen I married with her long hair fanned around her face. We were lying next to the rock waterfall on chaise lounges, trying to digest Mom's Crisco Cuisine.

Lisa's eyes were closed and her ivory hands protectively covered her belly.

"Would you like a glass of wine?" I asked. "I'm going to grab a beer."

"No, thank you."

"Well, I am having one or two. Mom's food isn't settling too well."

"It never does." She grimaced and shifted to her side. "We really need to talk, Tommy."

"I know. I'll be back in a minute." My intestines protested mightily as I started for the kitchen. I fed and watered the dog, desperate to postpone The Talk she was determined to have. My courage was bolstered when I glanced at my cell and saw a text from Kara. "Miss you. Soon, Baby. <3" I hit delete and extracted two beers from the fridge. The first was half gone when I returned to Lisa. Her eyes were still tightly shut and I wished she would nap for a bit. As soon as I sat, she blinked them open and fixed them on me, tugging at her shirt. I was a deer in baby blue headlights.

"Tommy, I know things have not been good with us for a long time. It's mostly my fault. I let Delaney and shopping and the house and my hair appointments take over. Somewhere along the way, you and I got lost."

"Lisa, that's . . ."

"No, Tommy. Please don't interrupt me. I need to say this."

"Okay." I shifted my attention to the beer and closed my eyes to listen. Maybe she wanted a divorce.

"I am sorry I've been so distant lately. Every time you come home I'm asleep on the couch."

"I noticed."

She stood and brushed the hair from my face, the most tender gesture I'd seen from her in a year. "I still love you, Tommy."

"You do?"

She sat back down. "I do. I want us to start over."

"Lisa, there is a lot on my mind, too. If you'll let me talk . . ."

She held up her hand, took a deep breath and exhaled slowly. "I'm pregnant."

I stared at her. "It sounded like you said you're pregnant."

"I did. I'm about a month and a half along." She studied my face. "Oh, God. You are not happy about this, are you?" She was starting to cry.

"No, Lisa, it's not—I am just kinda stunned. I thought there was no way."

"That's what I thought. I was more surprised than you are." She wiped her cheek with the back of her hand. It was shaking badly.

"Wow."

"That's what you have to say? Wow?"

"You've been to the doctor? You're sure?"

"Of course. I did a home test and thought it had to be a false positive." She shook her head and adjusted her chair to a sitting position. "It wasn't."

"I need a minute. My stomach is not doing too well." I went to the downstairs bathroom and splashed water on my face, staring at the mirror. *This changes everything.*

Some balding, middle-aged idiot looked back at me. A man who had been given all he could wish for—beautiful wife and daughter, financial success, good health, loving parents—and risked it all. An asshole. An asshole with a baby on the way. *Didn't see that coming, did you, Tommy?*

I returned to find Lisa standing by the pool sobbing. She fell into my arms. I pulled her to me, stroking her hair and whispering, "Everything is fine, baby. I love you."

"You don't seem very happy about becoming an Old Daddy."

"I am thrilled to be an Old Daddy. I may be the guy in the park with a walker, but I will teach him to throw a football."

"Him, huh?"

"Just a hunch. You know all I care about is happy and healthy." I took her hand and led her up to our bedroom.

Fifteen minutes later she was snoring softly. I pondered the shadows on the wall all night, knowing I would not sleep until I ended things with Kara. When the sun came up I kissed Lisa's forehead and went to cook blueberry pancakes. She'd loved them when Delaney was on the way.

I Don't Like Mondays

Tommy

I drove Delaney to her first day of resumed classes. The middle school was sharing space with elementary students until repairs were complete at Folsom. She was not thrilled about going back. "Are you picking me up or Mom?"

"Your mother is. She is taking you somewhere after school."

"Where?"

"It's a surprise." *Boy, was that an understatement.* "I love you, Delaney."

She threw me a kiss and turned to make her way through the crowd. The first-graders looked like wee aliens among the middle school population. *And in six years, I'll be dropping one off. Delaney will be in college.* I shook my head and braced myself for a rough morning.

Kara was slouched in the chair opposite my desk, wearing a black silk shirt and pants. Her heel waved impatiently in the air. I closed the door and went straight to sit across from her, wondering how to begin. Jeff Stephens was the only other person in the office this morning. With any luck, he wouldn't hear her crying.

"Kara, I didn't tell her."

There. That was a start.

She cocked her head to one side. "Why not?"

"Because this has to stop. I am so sorry, Kara. You know how much I care about you, but . . ."

"Stop? Why?" She interrupted. She was still slumped down in the chair, regarding me like a rattlesnake. *More like a paper target.*

"Lisa is pregnant, Kara. There is no way I am going to end my marriage. I had a lot of time to think . . ."

She turned her gaze to the carpet. "Pregnant," she murmured. I watched her trace a line in the carpet with her shoe for a minute. *Please, no hysteria.*

She raised her head slowly, placing her palms on my desk and leaning forward. "Fifteen per cent," she said flatly.

"What are you talking about? Fifteen per cent of what?"

"Of Aviation Systems, Tommy. That is the cost of my relocation. Not to mention my silence."

"You have got to be kidding me."

"Not one bit. I'm about ready to leave this hick town anyway, and I will do it with a fantastic job arranged upon your recommendation and some nifty paperwork from your accountant." She glared at me. Suddenly the woman had ice water in her veins. "I can describe every little thing," she paused and smiled slowly, "about your body in fine detail. I have photos on my cell, Tommy. There is also a record of hundreds of calls. If you don't want your now-precious wife and daughter to hear the tale I have to tell, I suggest you get busy with my requests." She stood and crossed to the door, gathering her hair into a ponytail. I now recognized it as her signature "I mean business" gesture. "I might like to live in

New York or Chicago," she continued. "Do you have any connections there?"

"No."

She ignored me and continued.

"My salary range is $125,000 to $175,000. I expect my share of A.S. in writing by Friday." She reached down to adjust her shoe strap. "Look at it this way, Tommy—a divorce would have been much more expensive and messy."

"Who the hell are you, Kara?" I stared at her in disbelief. "I thought . . . you act like this was your plan all along."

"Not at all. This was my Plan B." She closed the door softly behind her.

Now what? I laid my head on my desk. It was spinning.

When Kara entered my office Friday morning I greeted her with a white envelope.

"This is my fifteen per cent?" She reached for my letter opener and sat down.

"No, it isn't. It is a first-class ticket to Chicago and a nice sum of cash to help you get settled."

She threw the envelope on my desk and jumped up. "I told you my terms, Tommy. They are non-negotiable."

"Sit down, Kara. You need to listen closely."

She collapsed across from me and crossed her arms in front of her chest, one eyebrow arched in question. I noticed fine hairs on her upper lip for the first time.

"Your terms are off the table. I have made some arrangements with my wife's help. A close friend of hers from our IBM days has agreed to hire you as a senior software engineer. His company is a bigger success than mine. You will do very well. He is starting you at $150,000."

She sat up straight, eying me closely.

"He's gay, Kara, so you won't be able to stage your usual scam." I smiled. "Lisa contacted him on your behalf. I think that was very kind of her, don't you?"

"You told your wife about me?" Confusion crawled across her face.

"Of course not. I told her you had boyfriend trouble and needed to leave Alabama." I walked around to stand next to her. "Remember your dad's old friend, Wayne Sewell? I asked him to call your father and discuss your career history. You weren't very truthful with me about the circumstances under which you left Boeing."

Her head jerked up.

"Craig Sanders ended his marriage because of you. Three weeks later his son found him hanging in his apartment closet."

"I don't know what you're talking about, Tommy."

"Yes, you do. Gather your things and get out of here, Kara. You have five minutes before I call security." I handed her the envelope, noting she took it without hesitation.

"This is not what we agreed on. I can bring your marriage to a screeching halt, Tommy Robinson, and you know it. I can have Lisa on my cell in three seconds." She waved her iPhone at me.

"There was no agreement." I returned to my chair and allowed myself a laugh. "Don't shoot your mule, Kara."

"What the hell does that mean?"

"It means the key to your future is Lisa and her willingness to secure the only job you'll get in this industry. My contacts are extensive, and I know the truth about you." I pointed to the door. "Without her, you have nothing. Good luck, Kara."

She didn't even bother with the ponytail on her way out.

Among the Hobbits

Delaney

Our temporary school was a bunch of portable buildings behind the first grade section. Mrs. Gorey had us assemble in the auditorium, where she announced they were "the middle school cottages." I found it absurd that she expected us to call them that. She told us that Miss Ferguson was recovering at home and would be back in a few weeks. Mr. Bradley had lost his house in the storms, but he was seated in the front row. We had a moment of silence for Mr. Will, the janitor. His body had been found in the woods near Folsom Middle.

I decided the tornado must have taken my cheating accusation with it. Mrs. Dryden did not mention a conference with Mom and Dad. I hoped it was gone with the wind.

As we walked out for class, we saw the tiny red desks waiting for the end of morning recess. The playground was near the "cottages." We sat at our desks and tried to concentrate on English, listening to the tiny people scream and laugh. Our sub, Mr. Garman, was about a hundred years old and didn't seem to care about Alabama poetry.

He gave us a short story to read and plopped down to watch the clock, tugging his sweater tight around his skinny shoulders. He looked like he was freezing to death, and not too experienced with kids our age. Naturally, the boys in the back of the room started talking and throwing wads of paper.

Mr. Garman either ignored them or his hearing had failed. At eleven o'clock he handed out an assignment about the O. Henry story we'd read. He returned to his seat with a plea for quiet, shaking his head. "Get to work now," he said, "there are twenty vocabulary words in *The Last Leaf.*"

Hailee Williams passed me a tiny note. *"Do u thenk hell make it till lunch?"*

I shoved it into my backpack and returned to work. *Yes, Hailee, but I don't think you will make it to eighth grade.*

Lunchtime mercifully arrived fifteen minutes later.

I sat with Jami and Hanna at the semi-popular table. The seats in the cafeteria were little benches, and we hunched over the "pork chop shapes" and green beans. They were as disgusting as I remembered.

Jami pushed hers around with a plastic fork and announced, "This is crap. The food at Folsom Prison was better."

"Think of it as a diet," Hanna offered. "We will look great by summer if lunch is this gross every day."

"I'm taking this home to Beastie. He is not picky." I wrapped the donkey meat or whatever it was in a napkin and stashed it in my purse.

I missed my school a lot.

Mom was wearing a beautiful pink sundress when she arrived at three. "Would you like to go for ice cream?" she asked.

"Sure."

"How was your first day back?"

"Strange. I feel eight feet tall walking through the first grade hallway. The Hobbits are annoying. They stare at us. I wanted to stomp one."

"Since when do you hate little kids?"

"I don't. In fact, they remind me of my sophistication." I grinned at her.

"Ah, Delaney. My modest child."

"And your favorite."

"Yes, you are."

"Why are we going for ice cream? Have you decided to put on some weight?" Mom was usually very strict with herself.

"As a matter of fact, I have." She glanced at her lap and tugged her seat belt tighter. "This traffic is ridiculous. I guess it's all the construction people in town for rebuilding. Did they tell you when your school will be fixed?"

"Mrs. Gorey said she is hoping for the beginning of fall semester. Seems we are stuck in Middle Earth for the rest of the year. She asked for a moment of silence for Mr. Will. And Blabby Abby is supposed to be returning in a few weeks. We had a substitute they delivered from the old folks home. I think he might be Gandalf's father."

"Be nice, Delaney."

"Yes, my precioussss mother." I leaned over and eyed her with my best Gollum face. She laughed.

DreamCream was packed with people, so we took our cones to a bench outside. Mom polished off her butter pecan and waffle cone before I was halfway through my rocky road. Maybe she was taking up sumo wrestling.

"Delaney, I have something to tell you. I hope you'll be happy about it."

"I am sure I will." I focused on a piece of pecan near her lip and she self-consciously swiped it off with her thumb.

"How would you feel about having a little brother or sister?" she asked.

"We are adopting a child? Why?"

"I am pregnant, Delaney."

"Very funny, Mom."

"Seriously. I am due in December." She brushed crumbs off her lap and looked up at the sky.

"That is not possible. Aren't you too old to have a baby?" She turned to face me and I started backtracking. "I mean, not too old. You are still young. I don't know what to say. How can you be pregnant?" There was chocolate ice cream dripping down my wrist, and my mouth was hanging open.

"The usual way, honey." She stared at me, eyebrows signaling that I had better be respectful.

"Aww, *Mom*." I turned away so she wouldn't see the look on my face. "I don't think I want the rest of this," I said, jumping up and heading for the nearest trash can.

When I got back her head was bent over and she seemed to be searching the ground for something to say. I felt like a jerk.

"I'm sorry, Mommy. I am just surprised. *Really* surprised."

"I know. So was I. So was your father."

"Daddy knows about this?"

"Of course he knows, Delaney. Obviously I told him first." She patted her knees and stood, heading for the car.

I was right behind her. "What did he say? Is he happy?"

She stopped suddenly and whirled around. "He is very happy about the baby. We were hoping you would be, too."

"Do Grandma and Grandad know?"

"No. I figured the big sister should find out before they do." She tilted my head back, her finger under my chin. "You will always be my baby. You know that, right?"

"Now *I* feel old." I looked into her eyes and summoned my brightest smile.

She laughed and playfully waved the car keys at me. "Wanna drive?"

"Be nice, Mom."

"Yes, ma'am."

"Maybe we should go look at baby stuff," she offered. "That

would be fun."

"Do you know if it's a boy or a girl?

"No, it's too early. Your dad insists it's a boy, though."

"Do I get to name him?" I grinned at her. "I am thinking Bilbo or Frodo."

She thumped my arm. "Seat belt," she ordered, wrinkling her nose. "What is that smell? Eww. It's horrible." She pressed her window button and took a deep breath of fresh air, then clutched her stomach and started searching for the source of the odor.

"Oh, no. I forgot," I said, digging in my purse. I waved the meat-filled napkin at her. "I brought this for Beastie. Lunch was repulsive."

"It still is. Let's head for home. Please hold that thing out the window, Delaney. I'm about to lose my ice cream."

"I'm sorry, Mom." I put the window down and clutched the bundle of meat, letting my fist airplane up and down in the wind. I wondered what Beastie would think of a baby, imagining him sniffing around a crib and trying to climb the side. "What room is going to be the baby's?" I asked.

"I guess we will have to redo the guest room. I hadn't thought about it. Do you want to give up yours? It's closer to ours. That might be a good idea." She paused. "We could start from scratch and pick out new things for you. Would you like that?"

"I would love it. I think I want a black room. We could paint the walls black and fill it with white. That would be awesome."

"How about white walls with . . . blue?"

"No."

"Let me think about it." I could tell the idea of black paint was driving her crazy. She would give in, though. If I was going to be sentenced to life as a built-in babysitter, it was the least she could do.

As we turned into the driveway I remembered another thing I'd heard at school. "Meghan Reece says Miss Ferguson's face is messed up, with a huge scar on her forehead. That's sad. She is a pretty lady."

"Won't she get plastic surgery?"

"Meghan's mom is friends with her roommate, and she said insurance won't pay for it. Blabby . . . Miss Ferguson . . . is not sure."

Mom opened her door, pointing at the meat napkin. "Take that straight to Beastie. I'm going to lie down."

"Do you need anything, Mom?"

"Thanks, baby, I'm fine. I'll see you in an hour or so."

As she went in the front door a black car passed our house very slowly. A woman was driving. She had a ponytail and sunglasses, and I didn't recognize her.

I thought the lady might be lost, so I started to walk over and see if she needed directions. The car took off really fast and ran the stop sign at the corner. The license plate was from Tennessee: "PSTLGRL."

Homecoming Queen

Abby Ferguson

"Oh, crap. Just keep driving, Becca. Did you know about this?" I shifted the houndstooth baseball cap down to my eyes. We were a football field away from the apartment, and a crowd had gathered in our tiny front yard. Two students from Folsom held a banner reading, "WELCOME HOME, MISS FERGUSON!"

"Of course I knew, and I will not keep driving. I am parking this car and you are dragging that cast out for your fans to sign." She waved cheerfully at the people waiting for us. I spotted Luke Bradley standing next to Faith, holding a big box with pink ribbon.

"Dear lord, here comes my mom." I picked up my bad leg and swung it over, preparing to exit as gracefully as possible. No wonder Becca had insisted I fix up for the ride home.

"Are you surprised?" My mother swung the door open and a

cheer went up.

"Yes, Mom, very surprised. Is this your devious work?"

"We thought you'd like to see all the people who care about you. They've been waiting out here for an hour." She glanced at Becca, who shrugged. "There's cake and ice cream. Your dad is grilling burgers out back, and your neighbor made fried chicken tenders. The lady from Montgomery? Mrs. Morrison? She is very nice."

"Yes, she is. I feel like I'm in an *Extreme Makeover* episode, Mom. Like Ty Pennington is going to show me a new bedroom."

"No such luck. There *is* a cute man here with a present for you, though. I think his name is Luke?" She nodded toward him. He was wearing jeans, an Alabama t-shirt and a black cowboy hat. I had never seen anything more beautiful in my life. Faith saw me looking and grabbed his arm, heading in my direction. The kids parted like the Red Sea for their principal, giggling nervously.

"Hi, Abby. I heard you were into hats lately, so I brought this." He glanced down at the box and extended it awkwardly. Mom grabbed my crutch arm to steady me as I untied the bow. Inside was a black cowgirl hat with a pink beaded band.

"Oh, Luke, this is so sweet!" I said. There was no way I was removing that baseball cap in front of all those people. I turned to my mother, "Will you help me to my room? I'll be back in a few minutes everyone. Thank you for being here!"

Luke stuck his hands in his pockets and grinned. *Ty Pennington would look like The Hunchback of Notre Dame next to him.*

"Abby, let them sign your cast first," Faith ordered. I noticed my students had been supplied Sharpies in a rainbow of colors. Becca reached over and lifted my skirt so they could scribble. I couldn't read what they were writing from my vantage point, and wasn't sure I wanted to. Delaney Robinson drew and filled in a large red heart atop my foot.

"We have missed you a lot, Miss Ferguson," she said.

"I have missed you too, Delaney. I ruffled her hair with my free hand. I have missed all of you, and I love the card you sent. Thank you."

"You're welcome!" they chanted.

Delaney continued, "Our sub is about a hundred years old. We have to keep him awake."

Faith stepped in. "All right, Delaney. Let's let Miss Ferguson go inside for a few minutes." She nodded to Mom, who adjusted my crutch and helped me get started.

"I can take it from here. Thanks." I managed a wave at the sea of faces. I could swear Luke winked at me before he turned to help with the banner. I hoped they would hang it somewhere inconspicuous.

I opened the front door and inhaled deeply. I detected my mother's pine cleaner and Becca's chocolatey perfume.

Oscar Wilde Thing was curled up on my bed grooming his tail when I came into my room. He regarded me cautiously at first, sniffing my hand and examining my face. "It's me, Oscar." He jumped to the floor and began rubbing against my non-casted leg. I hobbled over to the mirror.

It was hard to fight the tears. The scar on my forehead was redder and angrier than a mound of Alabama fire ants. I put on my new hat and arranged as much hair as possible around my face. It was a huge improvement. I wondered if Becca had conferred with Luke before selecting the long black and pink floral skirt she'd brought. Probably—she was thoughtful and the most wonderful friend I'd ever have. I smiled at the damaged girl in the mirror, determined to look happy for my friends and students. *Showtime, Abby.*

I opened the back door to the opening chords of "Sweet Home Alabama." Luke was standing next to a pair of huge speakers and working DJ magic with his laptop. I laughed and made my way over to him.

"Do you have anything by Kansas?" I asked.

"Worst music ever. Why would you inflict that on these people?"

"Well, it *is* my home state." I tried to look alluring, batting my eyelashes under the brim of my new hat. "Although I don't plan on returning. This feels like home now."

The crowd was singing along. You won't find a human being in Alabama who doesn't know every word of the anthem, from "turn it up" to the very end.

"I'm glad to hear that. You know, before all this happened I had planned to invite you to my house for supper. Now I don't have a house. I'm living with my cousin Carl, his wife and three screaming varmints, two of them in diapers. Maybe," he tilted my hat up a tiny bit, "we could go out. What kind of food do you like?"

"Anything but oysters or liver."

"That leaves us a lot of options. I'll think about it and let you know Monday. You will be back next week, won't you?"

"Yes, I promised Faith. I am terrified, but I'll be there."

"Everyone knows that sixth and seventh graders are the kindest and most polite creatures on earth. Why would you be terrified?" He winked.

"Exactly."

"That hat looks mighty fine on you, ma'am." He smiled into my heart.

"Thank you, Luke. It was incredibly thoughtful of you."

"My pleasure, Abby."

He turned his attention to the laptop screen. "This one is especially for you. I'd ask you to dance, but I am as clumsy as a man with casts on both legs."

"Very funny. When I get this thing off in three weeks, I'll teach you."

Luke picked up his beer and playfully tilted it at me, grinning and training his big brown eyes on mine. When he saw that I recognized the song, he timed a sip to match the lyrics. *"Ticks"* by *Brad Paisley.* I was blushing from the toes up.

Faith had sent the kids home before the adult beverage portion of the party. That was a relief. I could hear the inevitable Miss Ferguson and Mr. Bradley jokes in my head already.

Hidden behind the screen, he mouthed the chorus at me. "I'd like to see you out in the moonlight . . . I'd like to kiss you way back in the sticks . . ."

Becca and her boyfriend created an impromptu dance floor by moving some chairs and began some sort of two-step. My parents amazed me by joining them. Luke moved to my side and whispered, "Next weekend. We'll get a little mud on the tires, okay?"

"Sounds good. What is going on with your house?"

He frowned. "They finally got around to bulldozing the lot last week. I have insurance, but it's gonna be hell trying to rebuild. I am not looking forward to it." He kicked at the grass. "At least I got Wilma out of there in time."

"Wilma?"

"Best blue tick hound in Alabama. She likes to hunt. Do you like to hunt?"

"For shoes on sale."

"Ever been muddin'?"

"No. But I have ridden in some fine pick-up trucks."

He laughed. "None as fine as mine, lady. Wait till you experience Big Red."

"Seriously, Luke? You named your truck?"

"Sure. Doesn't everyone?"

"I am not sure I can even get into a pick-up truck with this cast." I peered down at my leg, covered in middle school graffiti.

"Not a problem. Check out these guns." He flexed his biceps for me. It was impressive.

"Not bad for a math teacher." I grinned at him.

"Yeah, well, this math teacher almost made the Crimson Tide football team. I played wide receiver in high school. They checked me out."

"I'll bet they did."

"Would you like a glass of wine, Abby?"

"I would love one."

By the time he returned, I had decided on two things: Luke Bradley was even more fascinating than I'd thought, and Faith Gorey had definitely been working behind the scenes to get us together. I sent her a smile as her husband attempted to dip her to the strains of "If I Had You" by Alabama. I wanted my cast removed, and I wanted to dance. Mostly, I wanted to thank God for my friends and family.

There has never been a happier girl in the world than Abby Ferguson at that moment in time. Luke slipped his hand into mine and squeezed it tightly as we watched the people in the back yard flail about. The sun dropped behind the pines and Becca plugged in our deep red party lights on the patio. Mom brought me a plate and cup and set it on top of a speaker next to my wine. Fried chicken tenders and sweet tea, classic Southern healing food.

I turned to Luke, tapping the brim of my hat. "Do you think Faith will let me wear this in the classroom?"

"I already asked her. You and I both have black cowboy hat clearance. We will match every day."

It was good to be home.

Building a Foundation

Tommy

After Kara left I thought a lot about Aviation Systems and its future. I wanted to continue to keep the company private and ensure financial security for my family. Kara pointed out my vulnerability—had I not thought quickly, she could have handed me my arm and leg on a platter. *With relish.*

I considered what I had done to repay the world for my good fortune. Lisa and I attended the occasional fundraiser. We supported our church generously. I sponsored two local Little League teams. It didn't seem like enough. I was never going to be Bill Gates, covering Africa with a mosquito net—but I could do more.

Our neighbors were busy trying to rebuild their lives after the storms. Lisa and I went to the grocery store with Delaney and picked up a few hundred dollars worth of supplies to take to a shelter in Ohatchee, which had been hit hard. The local landscape looked like angry giants had descended, tossing giant oaks and stomping a clearly visible path. Skeletons of houses flew tattered American flags. Yellow tape boundaries were everywhere. Mountains of debris had been bulldozed.

The church housing the homeless was surrounded by tents. We had to get in line behind six cars delivering food, clothing and basic necessities. Some were neighbors and others came from hundreds of miles away.

When we got inside, Delaney and Lisa gravitated to a smiling baby with her family of five, all of them dressed in mismatched Salvation Army clothing. As my daughter entertained the little children with paper and crayons, Lisa took the mom to a corner of the makeshift "living room" to talk. I carried groceries in and explored the supply room. I was amazed by the stacks of donated food. A local distributor had sent several cases of gourmet candy bars, which were situated next to cans of pork and beans. Toilet paper pallets grazed the ceiling.

The shelter manager approached me silently, raking her fingers through long curly hair. "I haven't slept in twenty-six hours," she said. "I have three children at home, and a husband to watch over them, thank God. Thank you for all of this," she waved at my bags of tuna and toothpaste. "It's really touching to see people reach out." She extended her hand. "Sorry, forgot to introduce myself—I'm Charlotte Stewart."

"Tommy Robinson. Do you live near here?"

"Born and raised. Our house is about about ten miles up the road, and the storm didn't come near us. I volunteered to set this up with the help of the Red Cross. I'm kinda learning on the job." She sighed heavily and shook her head. "The thing is," she continued, "I am enjoying my work here. I think I may go through training and make a career of it. My mom always told me I thrive on chaos." She smiled. "I'm getting plenty lately."

"I bet you are."

"Did you hear they've confirmed that fifty tornadoes passed through Alabama? Ours was an EF-4. Those are usually reserved for the dust bowl or a Hollywood blockbuster." She shook her head. "It's going to take ten years for Tuscaloosa and some other cities to get back to normal. It will be an entirely new kind of normal for lots of these people. Several of the children here have nightmares, and I am sure the adults do, too." She glanced at Lisa and the lady she was standing with. "Your wife is talking to a woman who lost everything but the lives of her husband and children. Her grandparents were killed. Their church was completely leveled, too."

"It's hard to imagine what they're going through. We have friends and family with minor damage, but most of us came through fine. Our daughter's school was nearly destroyed. The janitor's body was found in the woods two days after the storms. We had a teacher badly injured, and a boy we know is going to be in the hospital for a long time. They are going to be all right, though."

"The best we can do is pray and try to comfort each other." She smiled and put an arm around my shoulders for a few seconds. "I have to get on the phone and locate more cots, Mr. Robinson. We're trying to move folks in from the tents as we can. Thank you for your help. Y'all be safe."

I handed her a business card. "If there's anything specific you need, please call me."

She glanced at it and grinned. "I will. Our food assortment is weird. Heavy on candy," she chuckled and pointed at the boxes, "and light on essentials. The canned goods you brought will help a lot. Thank you again." With that, she turned and sprinted down the hall.

I heard Lisa calling my name. "Tommy? We need to move the car. People are waiting."

Delaney handed the baby back to his weary mother and patted the heads of the small children who were clutching her legs. We headed for the door, a chorus of "thank you" and "God bless y'all" singing us out.

On the way home, Lisa said, "Look. We are behind power trucks from Florida and Louisiana."

"They responded right away, and restored electricity to tens of thousands of homes within two days," I replied. "Pretty amazing, huh?"

She was staring out her window at the empty lots where grocery stores and gas stations used to be. "Yes, amazing," she said absently. I saw a tear running down her cheek.

I spotted a big homemade wood sign propped against the frame of someone's former house. It was spray painted in red, "THANK YOU EVERYONE FOR YOUR HELP."

"You okay, Delaney?" I glanced in the rear view mirror.

"Yes, sir. Just thinking."

I turned the radio up and let each of us process the scenery in our own way.

A few weeks later Lisa told me, "Maureen Reece says that Abby Ferguson is going to need twenty thousand dollars for scar excision. Her parents don't have it, and she refuses to let them mortgage their house. She is such a pretty girl, Tommy, it breaks my heart. Delaney and Hanna are having a garage sale next weekend to raise money for her, along with several of their classmates."

I had seen Miss Ferguson, surrounded by Delaney and her school friends. She was smiling sweetly from under a baseball cap as they scribbled all over her cast. I was in a line of cars full of parents waiting for the kids to finish welcoming her home.

The school janitor's widow and children had gone to Ohio to live with his parents. A boy from our church, Chris Jackson, was going to require a long stay in a physical rehabilitation center in Birmingham. A committee had been formed to help. Ladies were taking supper to their house every night and getting the other children to and from school. I knew the collection plates would never hold enough money to make a real difference with his medical bills, though. His parents were being financially devastated.

All of this was weighing on my mind, along with the fact that I had been spared along with my loved ones and given a second chance to work on my marriage. *When God closes a door, somewhere he opens a window.*

I picked up the phone and called Margaret Higgins. She had been my accountant from day one, and I trusted her with every detail of my financial life.

"Hi, Tommy," she answered. "Y'all doing okay?"

"Very well, Margaret, thanks. And you?"

"Doing great. Tax season is over, and I can finally exhale. What's up?"

"I am thinking of starting a charitable foundation of some sort. Nothing too big. I want it to be completely anonymous and make distributions as soon as possible."

"You're talking about a charitable trust. How much do you want to set up?"

"Three hundred thousand. Can we afford it?"

"You can afford it. Let me do some preliminary work and get back to you. I'll have to get together with Dale Rice. No way to proceed without an attorney."

"I guess that shouldn't surprise me. Please tell Dale I'm in a hurry, and need to get this done way faster than in laywer-swimming-through-molasses-in-sweatpants time."

"Shall I quote you directly on that?"

"Yep." Dale was a high school friend of mine and wouldn't mind the ribbing. "Margaret? I don't want my name anywhere near the foundation. I want to call it The GM Fund."

"GM?"

"Private joke. When we issue checks the name will be different."

"Okay. I'll update you tomorrow."

"Thanks. Bye."

I drummed my fingers on the desk and grinned. *The Golden Mule Foundation.* My mom and dad would appreciate the humor.

I Will Always Love You

TOM

"That dress becomes you, Lily. Have you lost weight?"

She smiled and ran her fingers along the skirt, smoothing it as she went back and forth on the porch swing.

"Keep lying, Tom Robinson, and I'll feed you another serving of peach cobbler." She swatted at the gnats swirling around her head. "I wish it would cool off out here."

I could hear the television in her living room. All three grandchildren were huddled around it, watching some mindless cartoon. I knew Lily would have them seated with legs crossed and perfect posture, properly terrified to act up in front of company.

"What time did Millard say he'd be home?"

"He should have been here thirty minutes ago. The man goes to town and gets lost, I think. He's probably driving around aimlessly, trying to remember what I sent him for."

"Men are entitled to do that, especially without a written list." I scraped the last of the peaches from my bowl and held it out to her. "That was wonderful."

"Want more?"

"No, thank you." I patted my belly. "Ellie and I are going out to eat tonight."

"Y'all still going to the Sweet Home Cafe?"

"Yes. Best food I've had other than yours, and the buffet is only $7.95."

She nodded. "They were lucky the tornado missed them. It sure was close."

"Yeah, it was. I am still waiting to get my garage fixed up. Damned insurance."

"Tom." She waved at the window in front of the TV. "Language, please."

"Sorry, ma'am. I forgot about the kids." I had forgotten about her son Todd's being in the insurance business, too. Give me a foot, and I'll shoot it or insert it in my mouth.

"Where are you and Millard going off to, anyway?" she asked.

"It is a highly secret mission."

"Uh huh. Well, it had better not have anything to do with my birthday. Getting old is bad enough without having it announced to the world."

"You're getting prettier every year, Lily. The world thinks you're about forty."

"Thank you." She nodded vigorously and shot me a look. "There is a pig hovering near your head." She stomped her feet to stop the swing and jumped up, grabbing the front door handle. "Y'all better not be fighting in there, Carlton!" she yelled. "I'm coming in."

I had lost count of the years since she'd been in a classroom, but the woman could still bring order to unruly children in a flash. I found myself sitting up straighter in my chair and uncrossing my legs.

Lily herded her grandchildren onto the porch. "Say hello to Mr. Robinson," she commanded.

Sasha was a miniature of her grandmother, exactly the two-year-old in my memories but wearing a Spongebob Squarepants shirt and shorts instead of the frilly dresses Lily's mother had insisted on. She walked over and offered me a hug around the neck, smiling shyly. Her older brothers, Carlton and Mil, extended their hands for manly shakes. Mil was almost five now. Thank God they didn't make him go out into the world as "Millard." That kind of name can make a boy's life pure hell.

"Y'all go on and play now. Don't leave this yard, though. Mil, watch your baby sister." Lily waved them off the porch and settled back into the swing.

Carlton reached down and grabbed Sasha's hand as Mil bounded down the steps. "Can't we walk down to the lake?" he asked Lily.

"You *can* walk to the lake, Carlton, but you *may* not without a grown-up. Stay near this house. Your daddy will be here soon."

"Yes, ma'am." Sasha was tugging his arm, urging him to move on.

"And watch out for snakes."

"Yes, ma'am."

Lily sighed and looked down at the floor. I knew she was thinking of Daniel, and I kept quiet for a minute or two. Her first grandchild was born a few months after she lost her younger son. Mil had given her a reason to go on at the darkest time of her life.

"They are great kids, Lily."

"Yes, they are. I am blessed." She smiled, and I saw the face of the teenage girl she'd been so long ago. "Did I tell you Todd is opening a new office in Gadsden?"

"No, I hadn't heard. That is great, Lily. He sure has done well."

"They work hard, both of them. That wife of his is a good woman."

I laughed. "You didn't always feel that way, darlin'."

"Well, she had a lot of growing up to do. So did Todd."

"I think all of us are still growing up. We're just ancient while we're doing it at this point." I groaned and shifted my leg. "Millard is taking forever."

"He is moving around better these days, though. Since his surgery, he's a new man."

"I know. Amazing, what modern medicine can do."

"Uh huh." She stood. "Let's go inside to wait. I can start supper and you can sip coffee and catch me up on Robinson family gossip."

When I was situated with my cup of coffee, Lily began slicing a tomato over her sink. "I still look for him out there sometimes," she said, peering out the window. I could see the grandchildren around the play area Millard had built. Sasha was sitting in the sandbox, carefully scooping sand into a pink bucket and pouring it out on her foot.

"I know. I miss him, too."

"The dog is happy with Todd and his family. I couldn't watch him walking around here anymore."

"That's good."

She sniffed and dabbed her eyes with a paper towel. "Sometimes it seems like no one remembers Daniel. People won't mention him around me. I wish they would."

"He was a precious gift to you, Lily. To all of us. The truth is . . ."

"The truth is," she interrupted, "he lived longer than the doctors expected him to by many years. I know that, Tom. It doesn't make it any easier to take." She took a plate from her cabinet and started arranging the tomato carefully. "I was lucky to have him with me for all that time. What I don't talk about is the big empty space he left." She picked up a second ripe tomato. "It's like there is a Daniel-shaped hole in my heart. I . . . ." She stopped and grabbed a paper towel. "Dammit."

Lily curses are rare. I jumped up and saw she had sliced her left palm and it was bleeding badly. She was sobbing, too. I turned her shoulders to face me and she collapsed her head against my chest, her hands clasped between us. We stood like that for the longest time. When Lily looked up at me, she had stopped crying. Her eyes met mine and the next thing I knew, I was staring at her lips and leaning closer. I had wanted to kiss Lily Taylor longer than I could remember.

We were saved by loud screams outside. Carlton had fallen off the swing set. His older brother was crouched over him, yelling "Grandma!" at the top of his ample lungs. Sasha added a banshee wail.

Lily started, but I held her fast for a few seconds. "He's okay, I can see that from here." I loosened my grip and kissed the top of her head. "I will always love you, Lily," I mumbled into her hair.

She was out the door and by Carlton's side before I could embarrass myself any further. He was brushing grass off his leg, crying and pointing to something in the distance. I grabbed the roll of paper towels and walked out to join them.

Lily was reaching with her good hand as I walked up. I asked, "Do you need anything from inside?"

She dabbed Carlton's knee gently. "No thank you, we can fix this up with some soap and water in a minute." The makeshift bandage on her left hand was bright red.

The kids spotted Millard walking up behind me before I heard him. "Grandpa! Carlton's hurt!"

Millard eased himself to a crouch next to his grandson. "Naw, you're all right, boy. Let's have some ice cream before your dad gets here." He saw Lily's hand. "What happened to you, woman?"

"I did something stupid while I was slicing a tomato." She glanced quickly at me. "I'm fine." With that, she led the procession into the kitchen and began scooping ice cream for the kids. They sat patiently at the table, eyes large and hands clasped.

Millard asked, "You ready to go, Tom?"

"Yes, I am. Bye, Lily. I'll see you two weeks from Saturday."

"Y'all better not be making a fuss over this. I am warning you, Millard."

"No fuss, Lily. Just a quiet dinner."

"Thank you." She nodded her head at Millard and pecked him on the cheek.

When we were inside my car he announced, "I have no idea what to buy. It's her seventieth birthday. I want it to be extra special."

"I was thinking of something, but I don't know if there's enough time. There's an artist downtown who does portraits. If you had a picture of Daniel, we could take it over there and see about getting a painting done for her."

He looked out the window. "That would be a good idea. Probably the only thing in the world I could give her that she would really treasure." He produced his wallet and pulled out a photo of Daniel sitting on their porch with his dog, Rocket. "What about this one?"

"That would be perfect. Let's go see about it."

Meanwhile, In Chicago

Peter F. Darling stepped off the elevator and sank into the plush amber carpet of his hotel hallway. It had been a long day of travel, full of tiresome meetings and stale donuts. He glanced down at his swollen belly, reminding himself there was a gym on the fourth floor. His aching feet propelled him toward the king sized bed in 822.

At six feet four inches and two hundred sixty pounds, bed size was at the top of his hotel priority list. Business required him to be in the air and on the road three hundred days of the year. He was only forty-five, and found himself lost in thoughts of selling his shares in PFD Pipelines and living full-time on his quiet ranch in Oklahoma, just him and a hunting dog or two. He was lonely and most days he didn't want to shake one more hand or close one more deal.

Peter F. Darling was worth more than two billion dollars, the result of constant sweat for the first fifteen years of his adult life followed by shrewd expansion and investment. He'd dropped out of Oklahoma State against his mother's anguished pleas and never looked back. Now he traveled under the name "Otis Garfield" and avoided any ostentation in his life. Money didn't drive him anymore. He wasn't sure what did.

Women made him nervous. The only one he'd ever been able to open up to was Gina, his college math tutor. She was his girlfriend for nineteen glorious months of sex and laughter and never seemed to notice that Pete was ugly. He'd heard it all his life, enduring nicknames like "Lurch Darling" from third grade on.

Gina was the girl who saw past the massive forehead and receding hairline that began in his senior year of high school. Now she was living in Tulsa and married to a Wal Mart manager, the mother of four kids.

Pete went out of his way to hide any hint of his swollen bank accounts. If he ever met another Gina, she would have to appreciate him first for who he was: a beer-addicted football fan who avoided mirrors and clothing stores, bathing when it suited him and clipping his toenails on the rare occasions he could reach them.

As he held the key card against the sensor of 822's entrance, he noticed the tall brunette who'd been picking at a salad in the hotel dining room. She'd never once looked up from her book. As he polished off his chocolate cake she'd risen, stretched and tugged at her short black skirt. Pete had seen legs like hers, but only in magazines. He watched her sway her way out of the dining room along with every other male in attendance.

Now she was dressed in a skimpy exercise tank and shorts, heading for the elevator. He pretended to fumble with the key, waiting to catch a whiff of whatever perfume she might be wearing. She breezed past him trailing the scent of soap with a hint of coconut.

Maybe he would go work out for once.

By the time he located his baggy shorts and best-smelling t-shirt, he'd decided it would be best if "Otis Garfield" enjoyed the company of ESPN instead of the goddess in the gym. He piled his bulk onto the fresh down comforter, arranging the plethora of pillows and trying to remember where he'd stashed his Snickers bar. He got up to dig through his suitcase and came up empty. The mini bar was no doubt stocked with candy, but years of habit forced him to bypass opening its door in favor of a cheap snack machine.

He padded out into the amber softness in his bare feet and turned toward the elevator. He was pretty sure he'd seen the usual vending machine area.

After he pulled the second bag of Doritos out for tomorrow's breakfast, he inserted a worn dollar and found it repeatedly spit out by the money reader. The fourth try was successful. Pete turned and began the trek back to his room, having decided to utilize the mini bar for a splurge on beer and a water or two.

The soft "ding" of the elevator alerted him to her return just as he started into 822. He turned to see her down the hall dabbing at her knee with a tissue, bracing herself against the wall with one hand and hopping awkwardly in place.

"Are you all right?" he asked.

She smiled. "Just a flesh wound. I'm a klutz in the gym." She eyed his snack assortment before he thought to conceal it. "Is that your dinner?"

"No, these are for tomorrow. I ate in the hotel dining room. I think I saw you down there."

"Really? I'm sorry. I was absorbed in a biography of Bear Bryant." Her accent was soft and unmistakably Southern.

"Are you a football fan?" he offered, summoning his practiced smile and hoping for the right answer.

"Of yeah. A huge fan. I grew up in Tennessee, but I secretly cheer for the Crimson Tide and harbor deep feelings for the Saints. Do you like football?"

He automatically glanced at her left hand, which was bare. "You might say that. Otis Garfield," he said, extending his bear paw for her to shake.

She tucked the tissue into her bra and gathered her hair into a ponytail, gazing into his eyes like he was a movie star or something. She took his hand and shook it delicately, covering it with both of hers. "Garfield is an unusual name. Do you live in Chicago?"

He would have sworn she was batting her eyelashes at him. This was not possible, not with a beauty like her.

"No, I'm in town for a few meetings. I'm . . . uh . . . a traveling salesman."

"Oh. Well, I live in the city, but my apartment is being painted so I checked in here for a day or two. I don't know too many people in Chicago. I'm just a lonely transplant from down south."

"Nice to meet you, Miss?"

"Evans. My name is Kara Lee Evans. Look, I don't mean to be forward or anything, but I was planning to watch some old Monday Night Football on DVD in a few minutes. It tides me over until fall, if you'll pardon the pun. Would you like to join me?"

He would give up any number of body parts to join her. "Yeah, that would be good. Let me put this stuff away and I'll be right there. What's your room number?"

"824. I think we may even have adjoining rooms, Mr. Garfield. What a wonderful coincidence. Don't bother with your snacks. I brought half a Snickers cake I baked this morning. See you in a bit." She arranged her ponytail once more, revealing taut, tanned abs and a diamond in her belly button.

Pete dropped his key card twice hurrying into 822 for a shower.

Kara opened the door wearing a baggy Alabama t-shirt and conservative black shorts. Her long hair was loose on her shoulders. "Come right in," she said. "You smell wonderful. Cologne or hotel soap?"

"My personal mix," he replied, glancing around the room. She'd arranged two chairs in front of the television and placed the cake on

a table between them. He noticed paper plates and two metal forks.
A candle burned on the dresser, filling the room with an fresh-baked cookie aroma.

She was watching him. "I brought a few things from home to
make it more comfortable. I hate hotels."

"Me too," he replied. His eyes settled on something metallic near
the candle. My God, the woman had a gun. His instinct screamed,
"Get out NOW!"

She crossed the room and picked up the Luger, then placed it in
his hands. "I get nervous, being a woman alone. Don't worry, I have
a permit. I grew up hunting and shooting at my dad's pistol range.
I'm harmless, I promise." She paused and regarded him closely. "Do
you like to hunt?"

"Yes, I do. My dad used to take me. Got my first buck at fifteen."

"Wow. I'm not that great a shot, but I try. Maybe we could go
hunting together someday." She aimed the remote at the TV and
Hank Jr. began inviting his rowdy friends. "Have a seat, Otis," she
said, waving at a chair. "Let me find a knife for this cake and we'll
dig in."

Peter F. Darling was in love before the coin toss.

The Truth

Weston Robinson, 1932

Duane Ledbetter sold me the mule for twenty-nine dollars and the promise of fresh vegetables during summer. I reckon he needed some 'shine because that was a ridiculously good price. He handed me the rope lead and said, "He's a good 'un. Treat him fair, Wes."

When I got him home, Emmalee started in on me the way women do, telling me I was stupid to waste money on the thing. He did look kinda wore out, but we needed him to plow and I couldn't afford no better. I told Em to hush and tied him to the fence. "Settle in, fella," I told him, patting his sweaty neck. "We are gonna work hard tomorrow."

The next morning I was up with the sun. Had me a breakfast of Emmalee's biscuits and gravy, then I went to put the collar on the mule.

He was gone. His tracks headed off into the woods. I found him an hour later near the crick, grazing on soft grass.

I scratched my head, wondering how he got hisself untied. I walked over with a rope and looped it around his neck. He didn't seem to mind one bit, and followed me home with no problem.

After securing him tight to the fence, I grabbed the collar and started toward the mule. He gave me a pie-eyed stare and stomped his foot, pulling back on the fence real hard. The next thing I knew, my fence was broke and the damned mule was dragging a piece of it off to the woods. I got me another rope and went after him. He was in the same place by the crick, standing and swishing his tail against the flies. When he saw me coming, he laid on the ground and turned onto his back, wallering there in the grass. I hadn't never seen nothin' like it. He was just wavin' his legs back and forth in the air, rubbing his back. I couldn't get him to roll over and stand up, so I sat down under a tree ten feet away to see what he'd do next.

After rubbing hisself on the ground for a while, he got up and waded into the crick and drank some. I figured maybe now he'd come on with me, and he did. By the time we got to the yard I was hungry for lunch. "Em? Would you bring me somethin' to eat?" I yelled.

She didn't answer, so I tied the mule to a low branch on the nearest oak tree and went in to look for her. I told my wife all about my frustrating morning, but she didn't seem to be listening. When we finished eating I set out to get some plowing done.

I bet you done guessed it: that mule was gone again.

This time he had took off down the road. He was heading back to the Ledbetter place from the looks of it. We didn't have no phone, so I had to walk near two miles to get there. Sure enough, that mule was out in back of their house, grazing like he had no care in the world.

Dolly Ledbetter walked out, wiping her hands with a dishrag. "He ain't good about stayin' in one place," she said.

"Yeah, I figured that out."

"I'm sure he'll go on home with you, Wes. He's easy to get along

with if he thinks someone is gonna feed him. I'll give you a carrot to
lure him with."

"Thank you, Dolly."

She emerged from the house with a sad-looking carrot a minute
later. "I know y'all ain't got no barn, but it would be a good idea to
build somethin' to put him inside. He can untie hisself. Don't know
how he does it." She shook her head. "It's the dangdest thing."

"I'll keep that in mind, Dolly. Is your husband around?"

"Naw, he went to town today." She rolled her eyes. We both
knew "town" meant Leroy and his still up the road a piece.

"Tell him I am gonna want my money back if I cain't get this here
mule to plow."

"I'll tell him, but I think your money is done gone, Wes." She
went into the house, leaving me to coax the mule. He didn't even
need no rope. He was mighty interested in the carrot and followed
me home real cooperative.

Emmalee was on the front porch. "I see y'all are getting' a lot
done," she yelled.

"Hush, Em. We're about to be, soon as I get him hooked up.
Come over here and hold this rope while I get the collar on him."

"I don't know a thing about mules, Wes. Will he bite?"

"Naw, he ain't gonna bite you, Emmalee. Come on."

The mule had crunched up the last of the carrot and looked
satisfied. I walked up with the collar real easy-like. He didn't flinch.
When it was halfway on, he jerked mightily on the rope Em was
holding and ran off towards the woods.

My wife rolled her eyes at me the same way Dolly had earlier,
then turned to stomp into the house. I was starting to understand
why Duane was fond of corn whiskey. I trudged off after the
damned mule with yet another rope.

An hour later, "Percy" was all collared up with the aid of the oak
tree. I had decided he looked like the man who ran the drugstore in
town, Percy Oliver. We set to plowing and got us three rows done
before supper. I was real pleased with Percy and gave him some

cracked corn we kept for the chickens. I tied him with two strong leads to the sturdy oak and patted him good night. He reached over and nipped at my shoulder. It didn't hurt me none, but I wasn't sure if he was being friendly or hateful.

I was relieved to find him waiting for me the next morning. I didn't know if he'd tried to untie hisself, but it didn't look like it. He accepted the collar with no problem. We plowed one row before he stopped dead still and refused to go another step. I smacked him on the rump and hollered at him, but he would not budge. I went and got me a stick to hit him with, but that did nothing. He was froze up and would not go.

I left him standing there and went to get me some sweet tea. When I came back, I found that Percy had collapsed right where I left him. He looked like he was kneeling in prayer. I yelled all kinds of curses at him. He just stayed put. I hit him hard on his hindquarters, and he didn't twitch a muscle. I sighed heavily and went to get a handful of corn, which he stood to gobble down and followed with a mighty snort. I got behind the plow and shook the ropes. Nothing.

It was hotter than the middle of a cast iron skillet over a bonfire. I was soaked with stinking sweat, so I took Percy out of the collar and harness and tied him to the tree. I went to take me a nap, thinking we would try again in an hour or two.

Of course he was gone. I retrieved him from the woods yet again and he let me put the collar on and harness him, but he refused to pull the plow.

Emmalee was watching and she hollered, "I have an idea! Hold on a minute." She found something in the kitchen to entice him and brought it to the field. She positioned herself in front of Percy and spoke softly to him in nonsense baby talk. He began to amble slowly forward.

We carried on that way for two and a half hours, finishing three of the forty rows I was planning. When we quit for the day, I double-tied the mule to the tree and settled down to a bowl of thin stew Emmalee had been simmering since morning. I was scared to ask what was in it, but the taste was awful. We had been married for two years, and happy for about a third of that time. My wife informed me regularly that she wasn't a cook.

"I hope you know I have too much to keep up with around here without coddling that mule," she began, gathering her stringy hair into a bun. "You are going to have to find a way to get him going yourself." She seated herself next to me. "This stew is not bad," she said, smacking her lips.

I kept my opinion to myself, concentrating on finishing so I could move on and listen to the radio. I washed out my bowl and walked the five steps to our old couch, settling down to relax at last. I was asleep before I got the derned radio turned on.

The next three weeks were a nightmare of stubborn mule and grouchy wife. Percy managed to run away every other time I thought he was fastened to something solid. I could only get plowing done when Em came out there and pretended to be his mother.

As the days grew hotter and stickier, my wife started spending more time with her sister. Katherine would arrive in her fancy Buick and pick her up to go to Birmingham or Anniston. She'd come home with shopping bags full of things she said Kathy had bought her.

She told me, "I need new clothes for church, Wes. We don't have any money, and you should be glad Kathy is well off enough to help."

I wasn't glad at all. I needed a woman by my side, and mine was clearly out of control. Her sister was a secretary at the fanciest law firm in Anniston. There was no way Kathy was making the kind of money she threw around, and the Buick had to have been a gift. It didn't take a lot of smarts to figure out her relationship with the boss.

I focused on the field. Our income was buried in that red clay, sprouting for the prime grocery season. The chickens were fattening up. My days should have been easier with the mule, but I spent hours re-capturing him and trying to force him to work. I got more and more desperate. One day while Emmalee was off shopping I walked to the Ledbetters' and asked for help from Dolly.

"He responds to a woman encouraging him," I told her.

She raised a weary eyebrow. "So does every male in the world."

"I'll give you anything you want from the crop, Dolly. Just come and coax Percy into finishing the plowing."

"I'm sorry, Wes. I really am. I am too busy trying to keep up around here. Duane ain't no help, and the young-uns ain't either."

She turned to go back into her house, leaving me wringing my hands in the yard.

That afternoon I hit Percy with a two-by-four on his head. I yelled until my lungs was about to burst. He would not do a thing but stand stock-still. I looked out at the half-acre left to be planted and shook my head in disgust and defeat. I settled on the top porch step to rest and Kathy's car came into view, delivering my wife from her latest adventure.

Miss Katherine Hardy extended a high-heeled foot from the driver's side and waved. She was wearing a dress no decent woman would be seen in during the daytime. It was cut real low in the front and tight as a tick with a belly-full.

"Hi, Wes," she called.

My wife emerged, holding a notebook and a white bag filled with Lord-knows-what.

"Y'all have fun?" I asked.

"Yes, we did. Did you get that mule into motion today?" Em replied.

"No, I didn't. I cain't do it without your help, Emmalee."

She gave her sister a knowing look. Kathy looked down at the ground like she was embarrassed.

"Wes, I am not going to spend my days rendering mule assistance. You can burn up out here all day trying to fix your mistakes, but I ain't going to be no part of it."

"My mistakes? What the hell does that mean?"

Kathy smelled trouble and opened her car door. "I'll talk to you soon, Em," she hollered. "Bye, Weston."

As the Buick kicked dust at us, Emmalee plopped down beside me.

"I ain't happy here," she said, looking off into the distance.

"I ain't either, Em."

Percy pawed the ground impatiently, waiting for me to give up and remove the collar for the day.

The Real Truth

Emmalee Hardy Robinson, 1932

The man I was supposed to marry was named Herb Farrell. We was engaged for over a month, and planned to run off to Georgia when I turned sixteen. He was a handsome thing, even though he was a good bit older than me. I didn't care. I wanted out of my house and as far away as his Packard would carry me.

Herb owned two restaurants in town. I worked as a waitress in Farrell's Ice Cream Parlor after school, which is how I met him, of course. He kissed me once in the parking lot when I had just turned fifteen, and I was in love.

I reckon you could say I was innocent in those days. It did not occur to me that Herb was kissing other waitresses until I caught him doing it. I broke off our engagement and cried for a week solid. He told me Annie Ruth did not mean nothing to him, but I knew he was lying.

I was about to give up on finding someone to marry when Weston Robinson started paying attention to me. His older brother Lee was courting my sister Lucinda on the front porch most nights, and Wes tagged along when he could. He was tall and skinny, with big blue eyes and a nice smile. He told me his daddy was helping him get a loan to buy a farm, and he was going to be a success in the agriculture business.

Like I said, I reckon you could say I was innocent. I believed every word that fell from Weston's thin lips, and let him kiss me good night after my parents went to bed. Lucinda went off to live with our cousin in Atlanta the year I turned eighteen, leaving Lee and the rest of us behind. She didn't even come home for my wedding, which was held at our church on a rainy Saturday.

We moved right into the tiny shotgun house Wes bought, and he and I did pretty well at first. I had some recipes from my mama and a few ladies at church. I kept everything clean and washed my husband's filthy clothes without complaint. I let him bother me almost every night because I was hoping we would have a baby. I missed my little brothers and sisters. They were far from our place way out in the country.

We might have been all right if he hadn't gone and bought the world's most stubborn mule. He spent the small amount of money we had been saving for the future on an animal that did nothing but aggravate him to the point where I couldn't stand to be around him. He spent hours out in the hot sun screaming at the poor thing and beating on it, trying to bend it to his will. One day I got so tired of the ruckus I walked out and sweet-talked Percy into moving.

That was a big mistake. Weston decided the only way he could get plowing done was to have me leading the procession through rocks and clay, sweat dripping off my face as I wondered who was going to do the cooking and cleaning I was supposed to be working at as a wife. It got to where I started hating my husband.

My sister Kathy came over one afternoon. I told her, "He is driving me crazy. I cain't get nothing done around here because our whole life is built around that dern mule. All day long I hear him screaming at Percy or stomping off and kicking at the chickens because he's so mad. I don't know how much longer I can stand it." I started crying. "Wes is no farmer, Kathy. We ain't never going to have much of anything. I know that now."

She patted my hand. "It will be all right, sister. Let's get you out of here a day or two every week. You can go places with me. That will help." She drummed her red fingernails on the table. "Have you ever got your hair done in a fancy place, Em?"

"Of course not. I wouldn't know how to act with someone fussing over me like that."

"Well, next Tuesday you are going with me to a real beauty parlor. We will have lunch and find you a nice dress somewhere."

My oldest sister was the star in our family. She had a good job in the city and lived in a nice apartment. Katherine was always dressed real pretty. She was beautiful in ways I could never hope to be, and had a figure I would have killed for.

"That sounds wonderful," I said.

The following Tuesday Kathy and I left Wes in the middle of a tantrum and drove to Anniston. A lady at Clarice's Beauty Salon washed and cut my hair, brushing it into a pretty style. Kathy told me I looked like a movie star, and we were going to try on dresses next.

We walked all over downtown, stopping in the shops with the nicest window displays. Kathy grabbed my arm and pointed at a red and white checked dress in Wakefield's. "That would be perfect on you," she said, dragging me into the store.

Sure enough, the dress fit me well and made me feel like a princess. Kathy took me to the shoe department and a man slipped some red heels onto my feet. She bought every bit of it for me without blinking. I had no idea secretaries made so much money.

My princess time ended when she took me home. I put my new things away without showing them to Wes and went straight to the kitchen to cook supper. I listened to him yell at the mule the entire time I peeled potatoes and fried chicken legs.

"Wes," I said as I served him, "you need to return Percy to Duane Ledbetter. He ain't never going to work out. You can get our money back."

"No, I cain't. Every bit of it is long gone, and besides, Duane and I had a deal. I cain't back out because I cain't get the mule to plow. It don't work like that, Em."

"You could try."

"You don't understand." He slapped his fork onto his plate and pushed away from the table. "I am going to turn on the radio. Come sit with me when you finish the dishes, honey."

I did not want to sit next to him. I wanted to run away from that house and live with Kathy. I wanted to work at a job like hers and buy nice things.

Kathy and I went shopping a few more times during the next month. It was the most fun I'd had in my life.

One morning I woke up feeling sick. I splashed some cool water on my face and cooked breakfast for Wes, trying to smile despite the griping in my belly. He went out and started attempting to put Percy to work. I knew he'd be yelling his head off for me to come out and help within the next hour.

I put the breakfast dishes away and went straight to our wardrobe, pulling out my red and white dress. I slipped it on and looked in the mirror. That is when I noticed my stomach sticking out. It never had done that before. All of a sudden, I knew why I felt sick. I smiled at my reflection.

Weston was already hollering for me to help him. I felt dizzy and sat down on our bed. The temperature was already near ninety outside, and I knew I could not spend ten minutes in the sun without throwing up.

I don't know why, but my eyes fell on Weston's rifle in the corner of the room. I crossed to it in slow motion and shouldered the thing, feeling the weight and wondering if I could shoot it. I placed the gun on the bed and slipped my red high heels on.

I picked my way through the yard carefully, keeping those shoes clean. Then I pointed the rifle at that mule, the center of my troubled world. Wes screamed, "NO!" but it was too late. I had done shot Percy. My aim was bad and the rifle kicked me to the ground, ruining my dress. Wes ran to me and grabbed the gun.

"What the hell are you thinking, woman?" he yelled. Percy's leg had blood running down it, but he was still standing. Wes fired one shot at the mule's head and he staggered for a few seconds and collapsed like his bones had dissolved. He landed on a row of newly-sprouted turnip greens.

My husband marched into the house with tears streaking his dirty face, not even offering a hand to help me up. I brushed grass off the skirt of my dress and went to tell him about the baby.

Broken

Abby Ferguson

In my experience, first dates are either playing-with-puppies fun and full of happy sighs or running-from-hounds-of-hell horrible with suppressed screams.

My Saturday with Luke was more like petting an old hunting dog, comfortable and easy. We went the week before I got my cast removed, so he lifted me into "Big Red" as promised. We sang along to his country music as we ran every dirt road he wanted to tour. We crossed creeks and failed to find enough mud to suit him. I suspected he wanted to get stuck and show off his four wheel drive skills.

He never once did anything romantic and did not try to kiss me. I insisted on wearing my cowboy hat and he had his on, too. We would have been awkward as bison at a barn dance, so I was relieved. He ran through a burger place and bought snacks for us, then delivered me to my door by ten o'clock. He said, "I have to be up at sunrise tomorrow. It was fun. Good night, Abby."

That was it.

I was very careful to keep my scar hidden. My biggest fear was that he'd see it and I'd never hear from him again. It was worse—he did not see it, and I *still* did not get a call or text. He avoided me at school, arriving early and leaving the parking lot before I could reach it every day.

I checked his Facebook regularly to try to figure out what was going on. There were no clues there.

I had cherished visions of Luke helping me through surgery, standing by my side, kissing me when I woke from anesthesia, delivering roses to my room. I had written him into a *Lifetime* movie as the loving and manly cowboy who'd rescue me. I found myself pining like a teenager, composing sappy poetry and daydreaming.

> *Your eyes are moonlit pools*
> *I want to wade in*
> *To gather your secrets*
> *And your kiss . . .*

"What are you writing, Abby?"

I slammed my laptop shut to keep Becca from seeing that I had regressed to yearning adolescent poet.

"Nothing," I replied. "Some stuff for class tomorrow."

"Have you heard from Luke?"

"No."

"You will."

One week later he texted me to ask if I wanted to grab an early supper after school and watch some TV at my place. Of course I did. I wore my old baseball cap, thinking it might be easier to cuddle. We ended up holding hands for three hours on the couch.

"Maybe he's gay," Becca offered when I complained.

"Maybe *you're* gay," I responded.

"Only for ten minutes during Rush Week." She laughed. "I am

not a Lezzbun." That was her grandmother's term, and Becca found it hilarious. "Lighten up, Abby. He is probably going slow because of all you've been through."

He didn't call or come anywhere near me after that night.

It was more than a scar, it was a topographical map of northeast Alabama's mountains. My forehead was tattooed, "I almost died in the tornado." Every time I looked in a mirror without mentally preparing myself, I could not help but cry. The tufts of new hair were scraggly wheat sprouts. The only thing keeping me from panic was the knowledge that my face could be fixed by Dr. Edwards.

He ran his thumb across my forehead. "Abby, I can perform an excision. It's a complicated procedure, but in time it would be difficult to discern any trace of the scar tissue. I am going to send Tracy in to discuss our next steps." He smiled warmly and moved to the exam room door.

I stared out the window at the rooftop air conditioning unit below. The hospital in the distance held patients with cancer and terminal heart conditions. *Don't feel sorry for yourself, Abby. You are alive. You are strong.*

Tracy knocked and entered with a clipboard. She was a beautiful woman in her thirties, all long black hair, bedroom blue eyes and boobs. I wondered if Dr. Edwards had sculpted her from head to manicured toe.

"Abby, here are some pamphlets about scar surgery," she offered, barely glancing at me. "I guess Dr. Edwards did not go over the cost of treatment?"

"No, he didn't."

"Your insurance will not cover cosmetic procedures. The out-of-pocket expense for excision and aftercare will total about sixteen thousand dollars." She bit her lip and looked at me for the first time. "I am sorry to have to deliver bad news."

Bad news? I would have preferred a baseball bat to the stomach.

"Does Dr. Edwards offer financing?" I asked.

"Yes. In your case, a down payment of fifty per cent would be required."

"Wow. Well, okay. Let me think about this and I'll be in touch." I slid off the table and gathered my things quickly, hurrying to my car before the sobbing began. I had nine hundred dollars in savings. The sweetest children in the world had held bake sales and put up lemonade stands to present me with a check for six hundred and fifteen dollars in a school assembly last week. I could not and would not ask my parents for money. They were retired and barely making ends meet.

I flipped the visor down and looked in the mirror. Becca had given me a heavy, thick make-up used by accident victims. I slathered it on until my scar was somewhat flesh colored, then replaced my baseball cap and drove home, wondering what it would feel like to let the car drift into a tree.

I was curled up in a ball on my bed when my cell phone beeped. Luke's text read, "How did ur appt go?"

I snapped the phone shut and threw it across the room, shattering it to pieces and scaring Oscar out in a panic.

When Becca got home from work, I was sitting in front of my mirror and considering my options. I'd never found myself beautiful—cute or pretty on a good day, maybe. Sitting and staring into mirrors was not one of my favorite pastimes, though a fly on the wall might have assumed it was since the accident. I had prayed for the scar to lighten up. It did not. I'd prayed for long bangs to grow in and hide it. They were not cooperating, either. I had a wig catalog, but rejected that as pathetic. I jumped up and started dragging my scarf collection out, coordinating colors with my favorite outfits. If I could learn to tie them on my head artistically, I could leave uncomfortable hats behind and create a stylish oncology patient look.

Becca stuck her head in. "How did it go?"

"I don't want to talk about it. Let's just say I am stuck with a giant red glob on my forehead for the foreseeable future, and am cheering myself up by looking for new ways to hide it."

Becca sighed. "I'm sorry, Abbs."

"Don't feel sorry for me. I will start crying, and that will make me more hideous."

"You could never be hideous."

"It's something I accomplish every day. Hideousness and a smile." I wove a scarf in and out of my fingers. "He said I need about sixteen thousand dollars or so. They will finance, but I'd have to put half of it up front."

She frowned and dipped her head, pinching her nose in Becca Thinking Mode. "We'll figure something out."

"There is nothing to figure out other than whether I rob a bank, start a prostitution business, sell a kidney or fall into the lap of a filthy rich, profoundly blind old man."

"You might consider a career in stand-up," she smirked.

"Will you go to the cell phone place with me? Mine seems to have broken. It's a good thing I have damage insurance." I waved at the collection of plastic shards surrounding the battery.

"Sure. Give me fifteen minutes. We must remember to keep steamrollers away from your electronic devices."

"Noted."

I wound a pink and blue silk scarf around my face in a way I thought looked exotic and supermodel-y, telling myself it was showing off my cheekbones. I decided to drag Becca through a thrift shop or two later in search of vintage scarves. I would embrace being stared at for my chic fashion sense instead of my big red third eye.

The cell phone guy looked like your average sixteen-year-old geek and stared at Becca's boobs from the time we walked in the door. "How may we help you?" he asked.

"I dropped my phone and broke it. Here are the pieces." I extended the remains confidently, hoping he would have mercy on me. "I have the replacement plan for damage," I offered, meeting his eyes with my friendliest smile. "I'm kinda clumsy."

He shook his head and regarded the plastic arrayed in his palm. "How long did it take you to gather all this from the floor of the canyon?"

"Please just replace it. I am having a very bad day." I studied the floor.

"I'll see if we have one in the back. You got your paperwork?"

"Yes." I produced it from my purse and waved it at him.

He was back in less than a minute with an identical phone, calling me to the counter for information. His fingers flew across the computer keyboard and then the cell, obviously trained by many hours of expert video gaming. "All set," he announced, extending the phone and box.

"Thank you very much," I said.

"You ladies want to look at some protective cases?" He waved to the wall of accessories.

"Not today, Derek." His name tag was the size of a playing card, pinned prominently on his skinny chest.

"Okay. Be careful with this one. They don't crush well," he smirked. Then Derek focused on Becca. "You like movies?" he asked.

"Thanks, but I'm engaged," she answered with her sweetest look.

"Lucky man," he grinned.

As we headed for the door he called, "Let me know if your relationship status changes!"

"Will do, Derek," Becca giggled.

We blinked into the bright sunshine, and I spotted a familiar truck entering the parking lot. Luke sailed by fast, heading for the little bar at the end of the strip called Joe Ed's. A Megan Fox lookalike in short shorts, tank top and cowboy boots jumped out of the passenger side. I sprinted for my car, dragging Becca along and hissing, "hurry."

"What the hell?" she said.

"I don't want Luke to see me. He just drove by with his girlfriend."

"Are you sure? I don't . . ."

"I'm sure," I cut her off. "I need to get out of here."

He parked his pickup behind my car and slowly approached the window. I had no choice but to lower it.

"I texted you," he said.

"Oh, I'm sorry. My phone's been messed up."

"How did your appointment go?"

"Great. We're running late, Luke. I'm meeting someone for dinner. See ya." I put the window back up quickly and he stood staring at me for an eternity. The truck roared off a few seconds later.

"Why did you do that?" Becca glared at me.

"Did you see that girl? I don't need any more of his sympathy."

"Abby, Luke is a nice guy. You don't even know who she is."

"She's hot and she dresses like Daisy Duke. I am not an idiot, Becca." I shifted into reverse.

"I think that is a debatable issue," she sighed and crossed her arms, watching his truck speed off into traffic. "I'm pretty sure of it."

"I don't want to talk about Luke or my scar or anything else. I want to go home and go to bed."

"The self-pity thing is getting old, Abbs." She rolled her eyes.

"You're not me. No one knows what it's like to be me." My forehead throbbed everywhere except the itchy mountain of red. I lost an inch of tire screeching out of the exit and ripped off my scarf, throwing it on her side of the floor. *"No one,"* I announced.

"Maybe not," she said slowly, "but you have to stop being angry with the world. It's eating you up."

"And *you* are forever Jung," I snapped. "Quit trying to be my shrink."

Becca sighed and pretended to nap all the way back to the apartment. She took off as soon as I was in my room, slamming everything in her path.

Four hours later I woke to the last whispers of sunlight through my bedroom window. I'd been dreaming I was walking up and down a hallway, knocking on door after door and no one would answer. After a few seconds it occurred to me that someone *was* knocking at our apartment, very loudly and insistently. My first thought was Becca—maybe she forgot her key, or—my worst case scenario brain kicked in—something had happened to her and the police were here. I had driven my best friend out in a rage. I threw on a sweatshirt and jeans, quickly flopping some hair over my face and running for the door.

"Hey," Luke said. "I need to talk to you." He shoved his hands in his pockets and eased past me, depositing himself on the couch.

"Let me just . . ." my eyes darted to the safety of my room.

"No," he interrupted. "Sit down, Abby."

I sat down next to him and looked at the floor, hoping my hair was hanging long enough to do its job.

"I thought you were going out for dinner," he said softly.

"Nope. Plans were canceled."

"She's just a girl who lives near me who needed a ride to work, Abby."

"Okay." I continued to study the floor, focusing on a brown stain in the carpet.

"Why are you avoiding me?" he asked.

"I'm not. You've been avoiding *me*, Luke."

"You know what? For a while, I was. I admit it. You are so wrapped up in yourself and worried about your damn scar, Abby. Look," he sighed, "I don't care. Do you understand? A mark on your face is nothing." He put his finger under my chin and turned me to his gaze. I flinched instinctively. He brushed my bangs away, tracing my forehead lightly with his fingertips. Then he gathered my hair in both hands, smoothing it back and holding it behind my ears. Luke stood up, leading me along with him. His kiss was shy and tentative at first, exploring my mouth. I leaned into him like I'd never been kissed before and he circled my waist with his arms, pulling me tighter and tighter against his body. He tasted sweet. His lips were gentle and full. Each time they moved away I sought them out.

Every cell in my body was screaming and jumping around. He moved his hands to my thighs and picked me up easily, never breaking the kiss and folding my legs around him. He backed towards my room, and I didn't stop him.

Luke placed me on the bed slowly and softly, like I was made of glass or feathers. He stood and looked down at me for the longest time. I was disappointed, because I had wanted that kiss to last at least an hour more. "Abby," he said, "I have something to show you."

"Oldest line in the book," I giggled.

He went to the light switch on the wall.

"No, Luke, please . . ."

"Hush." He lit the room and came to stand at the end of the bed, tugging at his black t-shirt. His chest had a long, dark red train track running from his left nipple to mid-abdomen. "When I was eleven, a bunch of us used to swim in an abandoned mine that had been made into a reservoir. I dove in, showing off, and tangled with some fairly evil rocks. Almost bled out before they got me to the hospital."

"How awful, Luke. I had no idea."

"Well, it's a reason people don't see me parading around shirtless. And this is one fine six pack." He patted his abs and grinned, then sat on the edge next to me. "I am looking at you, Abby. I have been looking at you since the day I met you. You are beautiful, smart, warm, funny and kind. Any man would be lucky to be with you. Stop looking in the mirror and see yourself through my eyes." He leaned in to kiss me and I pulled him down. He smoothed my hair back again and put his mouth on my scar, then moved on to the side of my neck. He stayed there for a long time, just breathing, inhaling deeply. He pulled off the tattered Alabama

sweatshirt and threw it across the room along with my bra.
  And my heart was lost forever.

Bama Rising

Tommy

The voice on the phone was one of the best-known in country music. "How are y'all, Tommy?" he asked.

"Doing great. I appreciate your taking the time to talk with me. I know you're busy planning the concert, and won't keep you long. I need a favor."

"Sure. What's up?"

"There are three people in our town who were hit very hard back in April. Two of them teach at Delaney's school and the other is a boy we know from church. He is almost walking at this point, but has a long recovery in store. My foundation is going to be assisting them financially, and I was hoping maybe you could send me tickets to some front-row seats for the group of them. I know it would mean a lot."

"Yeah, we can do that. You want six, so they can bring guests?"

"That would be perfect. I already bought tickets for my family. Lisa and Delaney are very excited."

"Well, good. I am glad y'all will be there. Going to be quite an event. We're hoping to raise a million dollars for tornado relief. Calling in a lot of favors."

"I know. I can't believe the line-up. Brad Paisley, Montgomery Gentry, Martina McBride, Dierks Bentley, Sara Evans . . . plus y'all . . . . I don't think that many country stars have ever shared a stage outside of the Grand Old Opry."

"It's a great bunch of people, and that's just the beginning of the list. There will be some surprises. I'll have Shelby mail the tickets to your office, okay?"

"Thank you very much. I'm sending an extra donation in from the foundation, too. I hope you know how much we all appreciate what you're doing."

"We're trying. Lot of people hurting out there."

"You make me proud my home's in Alabama, no matter where I lay my head . . ."

"Lord, Tommy, don't sing to me. You are truly awful," he interrupted.

"See you this fall at hunting camp. There's a buck on your property with my name on him. Thanks again," I answered.

He laughed heartily. "If you actually hit something other than a tree this year, I'll sing that song to you personally. Wearing a pink tu-tu."

"I'm practicing. You're on."

"It's a lot easier to spot a deer when you're awake."

"I'll keep that and all the other harassment from the rest of you ugly old bastards in mind. Y'all only keep me around for my beer and barbecue."

"It ain't for your venison. Bye, Tommy."

I gazed out the window, smiling as I thought of Abby Ferguson, Luke Bradley and Chris Jackson receiving the packages the Golden Mule Foundation would be sending the following week. Then I bowed my head and thanked God for giving me the means to help them.

The phone rang and I thought he was calling back to comment further on my lack of hunting skill. It was Lisa.

"I'm on my way to the doctor's office," she said. "Just wanted to be sure you're going to make it."

Crap. I had lost track of the time. "I'm on my way, babe. See you in the waiting room. Drive carefully."

"I will. Your mom is picking Delaney up and keeping her. Maybe we can get something to eat afterward, because I've been too nervous to do more than nibble all day."

Today was the CVS to check for chromosomal abnormalities. I was nervous, too, but determined not to show it. Lisa and I hadn't dared to talk about what we'd do if the test showed something horrible.

By the time I walked into Dr. Anderson's waiting room, they'd already taken my wife into the inner sanctum. I was led to her exam room by a cheerful nurse who looked Delaney's age to me. She knocked and Lisa called, "Come in."

She'd had a smile prepared for Dr. Anderson and instantly dropped it when she saw it was me.

"Sorry, honey, traffic was bad."

"It's okay. I want this done so I can get out of here and start wringing my hands until the results come back. I hope it doesn't take long." She shifted her weight on the table and arranged her paper lap cover.

"You worry too much."

"Maybe you don't worry enough." Lisa closed her eyes and laid back. "I feel dizzy. I probably should have eaten lunch."

"Of course you should have. I . . ."

I shut my mouth and stood as Dr. Anderson entered the room. She was a pretty blond woman with a soothing smile and soft voice, perfectly suited to bringing babies into the world. She was good with my wife's worries, too. I shook her hand, grateful she was in charge.

"How are you, Tommy?"

"I'm fine. Everything good with you and yours?"

"Yes, thank you. Lisa, what's going on with you?" She smoothed my wife's hair back from her forehead, an ancient and maternal gesture.

"I'm lying down because I feel dizzy. I guess I haven't eaten enough today."

"You may feel dizzy because your blood pressure is up. We're going to start you on medication if it persists. In the meantime you are going to promise me you'll take it very easy and spend most of your days lying on your left side. I want you to cut way back on salt, too. We don't want to risk preeclampsia."

Lisa glanced at me, and I understood I should not mention her new fascination with potato chips.

Dr. Anderson pressed a green button on the wall and a woman responded a few seconds later with an ultrasound machine on a cart. "This is Molly, our ultrasound tech. She's going to stay while we do this."

"Hi, Molly." Lisa and I chimed in unison.

Molly pulled Lisa's gown up and slid her lap cover down, exposing her swollen belly. "I warmed this up for you," she said with a smile, then proceeded to rub gel on my wife. Lisa winced.

"Are you okay?" Molly asked.

"Yes, it's just nerves."

She patted Lisa's hand and told her, "You're entitled."

Dr. Anderson was exploring Lisa's uterus already. She flipped a switch and grinned as a whooshing sound filled the room. "That's your baby's heartbeat. Strong and healthy."

Lisa looked at me and I discovered I had a tear running down my cheek. I brushed it away and settled back from the edge of my chair, trying to look relaxed.

"Lisa, this will feel a bit uncomfortable. Just lie still and look at your handsome husband." I caught a glimpse of a long plastic tube in Dr. Anderson's hand and tried not to wince in sympathy.

It took much longer than I expected for the procedure to be finished. Lisa spent most of the thirty five minutes with her eyes closed tightly. She cried off and on despite Dr. Anderson's reassurances. I placed tissues from the thoughtfully provided box next to my chair into her hand as Molly stood silently monitoring the screen. I couldn't help watching her face for signs of alarm.

"All done," Dr. Anderson announced cheerfully. "You feeling all right, Lisa?"

"Yes. I'm not dizzy any more. I do think I might define 'uncomfortable' a bit differently from you, though." She grimaced a little.

"You did great. I will call you with results in about a week. Everything looks fine, but I am concerned about your blood pressure. Tommy, make sure she takes it very easy and call me immediately if there's a problem. Lisa, give up the potato chips."

"How did you . . ."

"There are crumbs in your hair." Dr. Anderson laughed softly and turned to me. "Do the two of you want to know about the sex?"

"We know all about it. That's why we're here," I responded.

More laughter. "Very funny, Mr. Robinson. Do you want to know if it's a boy or a girl?"

Lisa and I had discussed this last night. She was unsure, but I knew I wanted to be surprised. "I'll leave that up to my wife."

"No," Lisa caught my eye, "don't tell us. All we care about is happy and healthy. I'm already convinced it's a girl anyway, because the hair on my legs is growing slowly like it did with Delaney."

Dr. Anderson raised an eyebrow. "Very scientific." She washed her hands and turned back to Lisa. "You will probably feel crampy for a day or two, and you may have a small amount of spotting. Anything more than that, or if you have a fever, I want to know right away." She gave my wife a last reassuring pat on the arm and turned to shake my hand again. "I'll see you in three weeks, Lisa. Learn to love carrot chips."

Lisa wrinkled her nose the exact way Delaney did when presented with vegetables. "I'll try."

We made our way out of the building hand in hand, Lisa uncharacteristically quiet and slow-moving. I swung the car door open and helped her up into the seat. She patted her knees and grinned at me.

"I need a hot fudge sundae for calcium," she said, buckling her seat belt. "Meet me at the Burger Bar."

"Okay, but no salt on it."

"Deal." She leaned over to kiss me and I stroked her hair. No crumbs. "I love you, baby. See you there."

You've Got Mail

Abby Ferguson

Luke and I were enjoying a late Saturday breakfast of his biscuits and gravy. The man was wonderful enough to start with, and I had discovered he could cook like a pro. He said his mama taught him. I made a mental note to write and thank her.

Becca plopped a stack of mail on the table and went to pour herself a cup of coffee. "There are a couple of things in there for you, Abby."

The first was a plain white envelope bearing the return address of the short story competition I'd entered. My eyes widened when I noticed it was at least three pages thick. I tore it open in a rush, grinning from ear to ear. Luke glanced at Becca cautiously.

"Thank you for your excellent short story entry, "The Cycle." Our judges found it interesting and readable. Though it did not receive a prize in our latest contest, we encourage you to enter again. Enclosed you will find information about scheduled competitions.

Keep writing. Sincerely, Southern Fiction Quarterly."

"Oh," I said. "Well, that's disappointing. Nothing like starting your day with a form rejection letter."

Becca grabbed a biscuit and remarked, "Yeah. I've heard most writers submit one story and are invited to sign with an agent within a week or so."

"No need for sarcasm." I patted the papers. "Maybe I will frame this for my Wall of Rejection."

"What's the other thing? It's in a Priority Mail envelope." Becca waved her hand at the coupon booklets and utility bills. "I think it's on the bottom."

I pulled the strip across the back and extracted the letter. Three things fell to the floor when I opened it to read.

"Abby, your community loves you and wants to help. Enclosed you will find a check to defray medical expenses as well as two tickets to Bama Rising at the BJCC in Birmingham on June 14th. Bring a guest and have a great time. The Golden Mule Foundation."

"What the hell?" I picked up the check and looked. "FIFTEEN THOUSAND DOLLARS!" I screamed. "What? Who . . ."

"Let me see." Luke grabbed it from my shaking hand. "What is The Golden Mule Foundation?"

"I have no idea. Maybe it's a cruel joke." I looked into his eyes. I was crying and hadn't realized it.

"I don't think so." He examined the tickets. "These are front row seats. Alabama, Brad Paisley, Dierks Bentley . . ."

"I have to call my mom." I jumped up to fetch my cell phone. "I feel sick."

"Becca, this check is from your bank. Is it for real?" Luke handed it to her.

She raised her eyebrows. "Sure looks like it. The signature is from a local accountant. I recognize her name."

"Did you know about this? Who *did* this?" I demanded.

"I have no idea, Abbs. Seriously." She studied the check. "I can try to find out Monday."

I called my mom, who reacted with a predictable grain of sand for my happy oyster. "It could be some kind of prank, Abby. Don't get too excited until Becca verifies it's authentic. Who do you know who would do such a thing?"

"I can't imagine, Mom. No one. I've never heard of a Golden Mule Foundation. This is weird."

"Call us Monday when you find out. Your dad is in the car waiting for me. I have to go. I love you."

"Love you too, Mom."

Luke was on his phone when I walked into the living room, running his fingers through his hair. "I have no idea," he mumbled. "Did you sign my name?"

He hung up and looked at me. "I got one, too. Carl had to sign for it."

"Did he look inside?" I asked.

"No. I told him I'd be there in a few minutes. Let's go." He grabbed his hat.

"I'll meet you in the truck. Give me a minute."

We rode in bewildered silence to Luke's cousin Carl's house. Carl's wife Belinda greeted us in the driveway, waving the envelope. She was a short possum of a woman with a thick body, pointy face and small dark eyes. Her freshly-showered hair only added to the impression. One-year-old Krissy rode her hip adorned with nothing but a diaper and pink pacifier, slapping her mother's shoulders front and back as if working some serious Play-Doh.

Levi and Tanya, five and four, banged their hands repeatedly on Luke's door until he rolled the window down and yelled, "Step back, varmints!" They immediately grabbed his legs when he hit the ground. "Uncle Luke" was their favorite human being because he carried packs of Skittles in his pocket and handed them out when Belinda wasn't looking.

"Wow," he handed the letter to me. "This is unbelievable. Ten thousand dollars to refurnish my house? Looks like maybe I'll have a television after all. Pots and pans, too."

"You can't go to your house, Uncle Luke," Levi pouted. He crossed his arms authoritatively. "You live with us."

Luke swept him up in a hug. "You and your sisters are going to visit me there, buddy. We'll have a movie night with popcorn and ice cream."

Levi stalked off to the tire swing, pondering the offer.

On Monday morning, my students filed in with an array of end-of-year teacher gifts. There were the usual ceramic items with "TEACHER" emblazoned on them (I had a box for these) and a few poignant, heart-touching presents that brought tears to my eyes. Danielle Hollingsworth's mom had selected a "Bama Rising" baseball cap in deep crimson. Delaney Robinson placed a bouquet of chocolate and vanilla cake pops on my desk with a note from her parents.

"Thank you for encouraging Delaney's love of reading and writing. We appreciate all you've done for her this year."

The thank you notes were special treasures. My mother the Junior Leaguer raised me to write them reflexively. She would leave a dinner party with one gestating in her and invariably birth it for the hostess into the following morning's mail.

I looked at Delaney, swinging her leg and concentrating on the questionnaire I'd handed out. She was going through a slightly pudgy and awkward prepubescent phase but showed signs of blossoming into her mother's beauty. In a few years, the boys would be fighting over her. She nibbled nervously at the ends of her long hair and glanced at the clock. We were all going to be watching the minutes tick past for the next day and a half.

Becca texted me as soon as she reached her desk. "All legit, Abby. No way to find out who's behind it, but checks are good. Tell Luke when you see him in the teachers' oasis. Go call Dr. Edwards. I love you. <3"

Two weeks later Luke, Becca, her boyfriend du jour Clifton and I waited outside the Birmingham Jefferson Convention Center with thousands of others in heat that approximated the height of summer in the Congo. "Bama Rising" was scheduled to begin at 7 p.m. but the doors remained locked at 6:55. Luke and I had our black cowboy hats on and fit right in with the crowd. Becca had given us huge plastic bottles full of margaritas. Each sip helped me restrain myself from disciplining the kids running up and down the concrete steps.

We were swept up in a stampede and I clutched Luke's jeans pocket to follow him to our seats. Halfway down the stairs inside I heard someone scream, "Miss Ferguson!" Delaney Robinson was sitting on the aisle next to her parents. Luke stood behind me to keep me from getting trampled, but Becca and Clifton were carried off by the current.

I was stunned to see Mrs. Robinson in a pink floral maternity top. She struggled to her feet along with her husband, smiling and reaching for a hug after Delaney released me.

"Where are your seats?" Mrs. Robinson asked.

"Way down in front. We're the luckiest people in Alabama tonight," I said, "and I don't even know who arranged it for us."

"I am so jealous, Miss Ferguson," Delaney stomped her red cowgirl boot. "Please take lots of pictures, especially of Luke Bryan."

"Will do, Delaney," I replied. "Maybe I can get you a Brad Paisley guitar pick."

"That would be so awesome!" she shrieked. "Did you know we are having a baby? I want to name it Bilbo." She patted her mother's belly affectionately.

"Congratulations," I said, "that is wonderful. Are you sure Aragorn wouldn't be better?" I winked at her as Mrs. Robinson rolled her tired eyes.

Mr. Robinson spoke for the first time. "We're hoping her Tolkien phase ends before the baby arrives." He held his wife's arm and eased her back into her seat. "Y'all have fun."

"Thanks. You, too." We turned and made our way through the swarm of frilly Taylor Swift skirt and boot ensembles and sweaty old men in Bermuda shorts. It was an interesting crowd. When we were fifteen feet away from the Robinsons, I turned to Luke.

"Delaney's mom is always nice to me, but I don't think the dad likes me. He never comes to conferences, and hardly has anything to say if I see him in public."

Luke shrugged. "I've never met the man. What does he do?"

"Something with aircraft parts, I think. I'm not sure. Anyway, I wish I knew if I've offended him somehow."

"Don't worry about it, Abby. Maybe he's just quiet."

Our section was so close to center stage it felt like it should have been reserved for family. Luke and I looked around, trying to guess if the more glamorous women were band wives or groupies. A gorgeous blonde down the row wore the tightest sequined red pants I'd ever seen with a skimpy black Alabama t-shirt.

From Alabama through Brad Paisley we were on our feet dancing, taking short breaks to run to the lobby for drinks. Bo Bice did the obligatory "Sweet Home Alabama" and Taylor Hicks was amazing. Dierks Bentley and Luke Bryan had the women screaming. I had never imagined a concert with so many stars, one right after another. Native sons The Commodores showed up and did "Brick House." We laughed along with a recorded video message from Whoopi Goldberg and cried through footage of the devastation across the state. Alabama's Randy Owen told us their goal was to raise a million dollars for relief efforts that night. I had no doubt they would.

After four incredible hours all the performers came back on stage to sing "My Home's In Alabama" along with the crowd of thirty thousand people, closing the show with an anthem we'd never forget. There wasn't a dry eye in the house.

We rode home in the back of Clifton's BMW. Luke gently removed my hat and kissed my scar, whispering, "I'm not so sure I want you to get rid of this. It's a part of you, and I love everything about you."

I was momentarily stunned by the L-word, but recovered quickly and grabbed his face in my hands. "The scar is going, and we won't miss it. I don't need a reminder of tornado hell tattooed on my forehead. The memories are more than enough." I paused to kiss him. "And I love everything about you, Luke Bradley."

A week later he was by my side in the recovery room, clutching a weird-looking bouquet of flowers from the hospital gift shop. I blinked a few times. "It's over already?" I murmured.

"It's over, Abby. You did great. Here, eat some ice chips." He held the spoon to my dry lips.

A nurse loomed over me on the other side. "You feel okay? Are you nauseated?"

"No, I'm fine, thank you. Just groggy."

"You will be for the rest of the day, honey. We're going to let your handsome cowboy take you home in a few hours." She nodded at Luke, grinning under his trademark black hat.

"I love you, Miss Ferguson," he whispered. "Go back to sleep for a while."

Too Many Candles

Lily

Tom avoided me for weeks after that day in the kitchen and I was grateful. I couldn't bear the thought of how I might have reacted if he'd actually kissed me. We were silly old fools, both of us. I'd made up my mind we would not be alone anywhere again.

Tonight we were celebrating my seventieth birthday and I felt every minute of my age. I'd begged Millard not to make a fuss. I wanted to meet Tom and Ellie at our favorite restaurant, get it over with and be home by nine o'clock. Todd and his family had dropped by the house earlier and delivered a big arrangement of roses, Godiva chocolates and a card. That was fuss enough for me.

Millard appeared in the bathroom mirror, adjusting his tie with one hand and patting my bottom with the other. "You're as pretty as the day I married you, Lily," he informed my reflection.

"That lie is all the birthday present I need. Let's stay home and celebrate my fossilization." I fastened a gold earring and turned into his warm arms. "I haven't been pretty in twenty years, and I sure do like your nearsightedness." He pecked my cheek and I caught a whiff of Aqua Velva and chocolate. "You know you shouldn't be eating candy, honey," I said.

"I have no idea what you're talking about. Chocolate is my natural breath smell. It's one of the reasons you married me."

"Uh huh. Let's go."

The Sweet Home Cafe was full of locals eating every variation of fried food on earth. We were led to a private dining room in back. I glared at Millard all the way. As the hostess opened the door, twenty people shouted, "Happy Birthday, Lily!"

He was going to pay for this when we got home.

Ellie grabbed my arm and dragged me to the head of the table, where a pile of presents were arranged. I noticed a covered easel in the corner and prayed it didn't have some enlarged photo from my glory days on it. Lord, just get me through this.

One by one my old teacher friends hugged my neck and wished me well. When they took their seats I was asked to open my gifts. Laura had remembered my wish to take up watercolor and bought me a paint set. A group of six had chipped in for lessons at a local studio. Ginger, an English teacher, gave me a set of Maya Angelou books. My former principal Herman Greene and his wife had wrapped up a gift basket full of my favorite snacks.

It was all wonderful. No one said a word about the easel, and I began to wonder if it tied into the watercolor somehow. "Thank you all so much," I said, standing and nodding at each smiling face. "Y'all make getting ancient a lot more pleasant, and I am truly grateful for every one of you. Thank you."

Millard went out for a minute, presumably to summon a waitress. I hoped so, because the entire room was going to hear my stomach rumbling before long.

Ellie patted my hand. "You look so pretty, Lily. Doesn't she, Tom?"

"Lily's been pretty since she was three months old," he nodded. "Seventy looks great on you." He smiled and raised his sweet tea glass to me, then changed his mind and reached for his wine instead.

Millard had arranged for all of us to have chicken and dressing, my favorite meal. Herb and Betty, the owners and kitchen masters, had heaped my plate as much as possible and included their homemade cranberry sauce. Betty's mashed potatoes were covered in gravy. There wasn't a healthy vegetable in sight, and I relished every bite. Millard grinned at me. The man loved to watch me wolf down food, and could not understand why I stayed thin. Neither could I, but I was very grateful.

I saw Ellie stab and steal a piece of chicken from Tom's plate as he talked to his neighbor. It reminded me that once upon a time, I would have saved some tidbits in my purse for Daniel's dog, Rocket.

I missed my boy. I even missed that stupid dog.

The entire wait staff—some of whom I'd taught as children—filed in and sang "Happy Birthday" as they delivered my fresh strawberry cake. Somehow they'd gotten seventy candles on it. I blew them out fast, wishing happiness and health for my friends.

After the cake was finished, two of my former students came in from the main dining room to catch me up on their lives. Leticia, a shy girl I remembered for her constant silence, informed me she was going back to college after dropping out two years before. "I want to be a teacher, like you Mrs. Taylor."

That was the best gift I'd gotten. I hugged her and said, "Call me if I can help, and be sure to send me a graduation announcement."

Her friend Tanya showed me photos of her third child. She was twenty years old, and the babies had different fathers. I said, "They're great-looking kids, Tanya. I know you are a good mom to them." She laughed and told me her mother was keeping them most of the time. I was not at all surprised.

I was looking forward to putting on my nightgown and reliving the evening with my husband in thirty minutes or so. My watch read eight twenty eight. Right on schedule.

Millard cleared his throat behind me. "Honey, this is from Tom, Ellie and me." I turned in my chair and gasped along with everyone else as he lifted the cloth, revealing a beautiful portrait of my Daniel. I heard someone sobbing and realized it was me.

"Aww, honey, don't cry." Millard stood me up and walked me over for a closer look. "We thought you would love it."

"I do. I'm just stunned. You all had this painted? They even got Rocket right." I brushed my fingers along the oil paint. "Daniel was so beautiful." I couldn't stop crying. Ellie appeared at my side.

"He was a precious gift to all of us, Lily. Where are you going to hang this?" She glanced nervously at Tom.

"In the living room. I know the perfect spot. Thank you all so much." I wiped my tears and turned to face the crowd. Each face was struggling between awkward concern and forced cheerfulness. "It's been my best birthday ever, y'all. Thank you for your kindness. I think Millard and I will head home now." I was immediately overwhelmed with hugs from folks trying to exit gracefully. When Ellen, Tom, my husband and I were left alone in the room, I turned to the portrait and traced Daniel's sweet face with my finger. "Thank you. This is the perfect gift for me."

"We all miss him, Lily," Tom offered. He picked up the painting and Ellen gathered my gifts as Millard went to start the car.

Bed Time

Lisa

I rolled onto my right side for a change of pace, plucking a stray hair off the pillow and wondering how long a human can endure resting uncomfortably. This morning I'd mentally redecorated our bedroom several times and brainstormed exercise routines I could do with the baby in tow. On my last visit Dr. Anderson informed me, "At twenty weeks you've surpassed your full-term weight with Delaney." Most days I squeezed into my old maternity bathing suit and waddled to the pool to swim a few laps, but even short walks made my back ache and my cankles required constant elevation.

I spotted some strappy red stilettos in our open closet taunting me and my swollen feet. Yesterday's mail brought neon pink Converse sneakers in a size 9 Wide from my mother. They looked like Barbie hovercraft, but my tattered rhinestone flip flops were the only alternative. Mother's note: "These will be great with your denim romper and the floral top I sent." I wondered briefly if I owned a rubber clown nose to complete the ensemble.

Last night Delaney had delicately painted my toenails in "Ballet Slippers," a cruel joke in itself.

"Hey," I'd asked her. "You know how you hide an elephant?"

She glanced up from her task, brush in hand. "No, Mom."

"You paint her toenails primary colors and put her in a bag of M&Ms."

"Maybe that would be better," she'd offered not-so-sweetly.

I'd glared at her over my expanse of belly, trying to arrange my hair prettily on the back of the couch. At least my hair was thriving. It was about the only thing left I could bear to observe in the mirror.

I sighed and shifted back to my left side, closing my eyes and trying to sleep while the baby wasn't soccer practicing. Her goal had been my rib cage for several days.

My stomach grumbled and I wondered if we had Pop Tarts. Maybe I'd be the mom at the park in a stylish billowy caftan.

Ellen was dropping by regularly with casseroles for Tommy and Delaney, and I thought I heard her downstairs. Beastie barked and I sat up and braced for a knock at the door. It flew open and Tommy breezed in with a huge polka dotted gift bag.

He kissed my forehead and patted my belly. "How's Tommy Junior?"

"We've had this discussion. The baby is Margaret Elizabeth, and we're going to call her Maggie."

"You're going to make it hard on him as a quarterback with that name."

He plopped next to me, obviously pleased with himself. "Thought you might like this." He pulled out a new laptop and placed it on the bed. "And these." Five of my favorite movies and a DVD of old *Friends* episodes emerged from the bag. "I set it up yesterday at work. You're fully charged for eight hours of entertainment." He tapped the shiny black computer cover with a worn fingernail.

"You are the best husband in the world. Thank you, honey." I kissed him, tasting coffee and powdered sugar doughnut.

"I'm trying. You take it easy. Are you still planning to go to the grocery store on your way to get Delaney?" He looked mildly worried and I wondered how puffy my face was.

"Yes, and I'll be fine. It's the highlight of the day I've planned. I'm going to smile at everyone and try not to look like something ready to shimmy into the ocean in search of plankton."

"You look beautiful, Lisa. You are glowing and growing our baby."

"Uh huh. Thank you for the wonderful gift. My morning is now a lot more bearable. I love you."

"I love you too." He was halfway out the door when he turned and added, "Are you hungry?" There was no way he'd missed the giant Snickers wrapper on my bedside table.

I lied. "No, not at all. I'll eat a salad when I get home this afternoon. Bye, babe."

"I'll be home by four thirty."

"Okay."

I had two hours before "Piggly Wobbly Goes To The Piggly Wiggly." The computer fired up quickly and I inserted the first DVD. Skinny people having fun in New York City. It was amusing to try to imagine a gargantuan Jennifer Aniston carrying quadruplets instead of frolicking in Ralph Lauren miniskirts.

I was standing in the produce aisle getting ready to grab some carrot sticks and bags of spinach. My back hurt more than usual and I was focused on ignoring it. I would finish grocery shopping, pick Delaney up and crawl back into bed, obediently lying on my left side and watching the season finale of a very green and enthusiastic *Friends* cast. I reached forward and was seized by a terrible cramp in my lower belly. I hurried off toward the ladies' room, abandoning my cart. The next thing I remember was Mrs. McIntyre, the elderly 'sample lady' patting my cheek and asking, "Mrs. Robinson? Are you all right? Do you need help?"

Her white hair was in its usual tight bun, blue eyes sparkling kindly with concern and a nervous smile displaying a pearly row of dentures. She glanced anxiously over her shoulder at the gathering crowd.

I found myself leaning against a wall with a group of three male employees and a woman I'd never seen a few feet away, staring hard. I looked down and saw blood had trickled down my legs, staining the tops of my sneakers and thoroughly embarrassing me. Mrs. McIntyre offered her arm. The pain in my abdomen was excruciating.

She helped me hobble into the ladies' room, pausing to yell, "Call 911. She needs to get to a hospital!"

"No, I'm fine," I insisted.

She locked the restroom door.

"You are not, honey. How far along are you?"

"About six months."

"Who is your doctor?"

"Renee Anderson. Look, I just need to clean myself up . . ." I doubled over in pain.

"What is your husband's phone number?"

I couldn't seem to get to a stall and slumped against the nearest sink, reciting Tommy's cell number. I braced myself there, crying and praying for a miracle. Mrs. McIntyre kept telling me to stay awake and talk to her.

I was wide awake. *Please God, don't let me lose the baby. Please.*

I had never been in an ambulance.

A young woman's face hovered over me, dark brown curls and huge green eyes. "I'm Elena. You're doing fine, Mrs. Robinson. We'll be at the hospital in a few minutes." There was a cuff on my arm and she glanced at a monitor. I couldn't see, but knew my blood pressure must be registering very high.

"Did someone call my husband?"

"He's meeting us there."

"Am I losing my baby?"

"Not if we can help it. Hang on. I want you to breathe deeply."

I was trying.

"Do you have a history of miscarriage?"

"No."

"Is this the first bleeding you've experienced with this pregnancy?"

"Yes."

"You're doing great. Just relax." Elena sat back and sighed. The siren wailed in my ears. I knew it was time to get Delaney at school, and wondered who would do it. She would be terrified when I didn't show up.

"It hurts so bad. I feel like I'm in labor," I told her.

"You're having pre-term contractions. You'll get medicine in the ER to help."

"Did I lose much blood?"

"No. Only a little. Don't worry about the bleeding."

"Are you monitoring the baby?"

"The baby's heartbeat is strong." She adjusted the strap circling my belly.

I closed my eyes and tried to block out the bumps in the road. It felt like the driver was detouring through the world's most uneven cornfield.

Tommy met us at the emergency room entrance looking cool, calm and collected. He leaned over and kissed me.

I was feeling much better and hadn't had pain for several minutes. "This is an overreaction," I told him. "I'm fine. I need to get home and lie down."

"Dr. Anderson is delivering a baby and knows you're here," he replied. "Her service said she'll come down as soon as she can."

Elena and the driver unloaded me and I was taken to an examining room. Tommy waited outside as a cheerful older nurse helped me out of my clothes. "Dr. Kerry will be in soon to examine you," she informed me. "I'll send your husband in to keep you company."

"Thank you. Wait, not Dr. Anderson?"

"She's busy, but will be here as soon as possible. Dr. Kerry is in charge until then." I thought she looked sympathetic for a moment. "He's new, but very good."

Dr. Keith Kerry was over six and a half feet tall and looked like an emaciated long distance runner. He wore his long brown hair in a neat ponytail, and could not possibly have been out of medical school for more than a week.

"Are you still feeling contractions, Mrs. Robinson?" He was very matter-of-fact and detached, flipping through my chart as he talked. There was almost no eye contact with me or Tommy. I wanted Dr. Anderson and her bedside manner in the worst way.

"Not for a while now."

"We're going to give you magnesium sulfate to make sure they stop. The nurse will be in shortly. I'm also starting you on blood pressure medication."

I glanced at Tommy. "Are you keeping her here?" he asked.

"Dr. Anderson will make that decision. She will see you in a bit." He was gone, trailing disinterest and boredom. No doubt he had more urgent cases to explore.

Tommy pulled the thin cotton blanket up to my shoulders. "Do you need anything?"

"I want to go home. Did your mom get Delaney?"

"Yes, she's fine."

I settled back and tried to calm myself by counting stained ceiling tiles as I listened to the fetal monitor beep. Tommy tapped his foot impatiently and the baby began a slow stomp in unison with her father's rhythm. Not a word was spoken. We waited and eavesdropped on the busy emergency staff outside the door. I heard an annoyed Dr. Kerry tell a screaming child, "Stop crying, it's not that bad!"and hoped he wasn't considering a career in pediatric medicine.

Dr. Anderson showed up about an hour later, looking freshly scrubbed and happy. "Sorry about the delay, Lisa," she began. "Twins wait for no one."

"What a wonderful job you have." I remembered my childhood dream of delivering babies, crushed in high school chemistry class.

"Yes, it is." She began examining me, Tommy clutching my hand and wincing each time I did.

An ultrasound followed and Dr. Anderson told us, "You have placenta previa." She turned the screen toward me, but it depicted only vague blobs from my view. "The bleeding was minor, but you are going to have to stay in bed for the next few months. We'll keep you here tonight for observation. If the contractions subside, I'll send you home tomorrow."

"What is placenta previa?" Tommy was suddenly paying very close attention.

"At this point," she responded, "the placenta is not where it should be. It's positioned too low, on top of Lisa's cervix. If that's the case nearer her delivery date, we will schedule a C-section." She paused. "Your blood pressure is way too high, Lisa. You'll need to continue to take medication. If we have more contractions or bleeding, there are treatments for that as well." She washed her hands and turned back to face us. "We have to be very careful and watch you and the baby closely. No sex, of course." Her eyes traveled to Tommy, who responded by directing his gaze to the floor. "And you only get out of bed to visit the bathroom or your doctor's office, Lisa."

"It's that serious?" I couldn't help the tears, and swiped my face with the back of my left, IV-free hand.

She nodded with a reassuring look. I noticed her smile did not reach her eyes. "The last thing you need to do is worry. We'll take good care of you and the baby. I'll see you on rounds tomorrow and decide if you can go home."

"Dr. Anderson?"

"Yes?"

"Am I going to lose the baby? What are the odds? How big a complication is this?"

"Slow down, Lisa," she patted my foot. "We are going to take one day at a time. You need to concentrate on trying to relax."

I could tell that was the best non-answer I was going to get. Tommy rose and followed her out of the room, anxiety scrawled all over his face. The man never could play poker.

They wheeled me to the fourth floor in a chair instead of a gurney.

An older lady from our church, Geneva Turner, spotted me and hurried to my side, patting her helmet hair into place. The hospital orderly dutifully glided me to a stop. "Oh, honey, is it time? I am so excited for you! As soon as that baby is born, you have Tommy call me and we'll get it in the bulletin. Does Reverend Miller know you're here? This is wonderful. I . . ."

She noticed my husband's head shaking slowly back and forth. "Oh," she sputtered. "Is everything all right?"

"Just a little bed rest overnight, Geneva," Tommy assured her. "Lisa needs to slow down." He paused for a few seconds. "She's supposed to be sleeping, so no visitors allowed."

I appreciated his improvisational skill.

She took my hand gently and said, "I will pray for you."

"Thank you. Please do."

The chair began its forward motion and I waved at Mrs. Turner, smiling at her like a woman without a care in the world.

Tommy and Delaney showed up a few minutes after my grilled chicken, salad and jello feast. They brought my laptop and a huge bouquet of pink roses. My daughter handed me a card she'd made with colored pencils. "To The Best Mom In The World" was situated among her renderings of grassy meadows and a blue sky. Inside she'd written, "I love you so much, Mommy. Get better soon. Little

Baby Frodo needs you to be strong. Come back to The Shire. We miss you."

I grabbed and hugged her, inhaling strawberry shampoo and recently-held Beastie. Delaney could make me laugh no matter what the circumstances. We started giggling and couldn't stop, causing me to snort loudly for our daughter's amusement. Tommy rolled his eyes theatrically but I knew he was relieved.

"Here," I offered her the plastic spoon, "I saved you some yummy green jello."

"Thanks, Mom, but Daddy promised me ice cream on the way home. I'm holding out for the good stuff."

"You people are mean, taunting me with thoughts of butter pecan heaven."

"I can go get you some," Tommy offered. "Want me to?"

"No thanks. I'm watching my figure." This led Delaney's gaze to my mountainous midriff and a new round of giggles. "Don't laugh, young lady. It's either that, or I hire a seamstress to let out my shower curtain and bed sheets."

She turned to her dad. "She's fine. We should let her watch her DVDs and go to sleep while she's still in a good mood."

When did she grow up so fast?

"Delaney's right, babe. You two go eat ice cream and burgers and fries and all my other food fantasies. I'll be right here resting, and you can get me tomorrow."

"Did Dr. Anderson come by?"

"No, but I'm sure she'll release me. I haven't had any pain at all. There's no reason I can't come home and terrorize my family with endless demands. The nurses are already tired of me."

"I'll get you a bedside bell to ring," Tommy offered.

"And I will use it. A lot." I pulled Delaney closer. "Give me a kiss, Gollum."

"Sure, my preciousssss motherrrr." She pecked my cheek as a lady in volunteer stripes entered the room.

"Do you need anything, Mrs. Robinson?" she asked.

"No, thank you. I have everything I need." I winked at Tommy and allowed myself a single tear of gratitude.

"Looks like it to me," she grinned. "I'll just take that tray. Want some ice chips?"

"Yes, please. The most fattening ones you have."

She laughed as she opened the door. "Your mom is pretty funny," she told Delaney.

"You have no idea," my daughter answered.

The Mule Has Landed

Tommy

I was exhausted by the time I got to O'Hare, gathered my luggage and hailed a taxi. The Iranian driver made several attempts at discussion, but his passenger was singularly focused on getting to the hotel and calling his wife before rushing to a dinner meeting.

"You come to city first time?"

"No, I've been here many times."

"You sound an accent like the South, no?"

"Yes, I'm from Alabama."

"Oh, Alabama. Creemson Tide, yes?"

"Yes."

I winced as Mahmoud/Adbul/Reza swerved around an old lady pushing a shopping cart.

"I keep taxi very clean."

"Yes, you do. It actually smells nice in here."

"My wife, she gives me spray to make smell of flowers."

"Good." I estimated I had twelve minutes of forced conversation before the Waldorf. I leaned back and closed my eyes, hoping the driver would note my exhaustion.

After three blissful minutes, my hopes were dashed. "You look now and see the skyline. That way," he waved his hand, "is the building of Oprah."

"Wow," I replied. "That's great."

"Woman can be very successful in this country, no? I tell my wife. She only want to be home with the baby."

"My wife is expecting a baby in a few months."

"Oh, congratulations. May you be blessed with a fine healthy son."

I ignored the implication and took out my laptop.

Seven peaceful minutes later Mohmoud/Abdul/Reza swung the taxi toward the check-in area and a bellman approached. I tipped the cabbie a twenty for shutting up.

"Here is card. You call if you need ride."

"Sure thing. Thanks."

My room was the usual king suite. I sank onto the bed and phoned my wife.

"Are you resting, baby?"

"I'm on the couch," Lisa replied. "Delaney is delivering my second tomato sandwich in a minute. I'm fine. I love you."

"I'll call you after dinner. I love you. Kiss our daughter for me."

Howard Elliott had chosen one of the most outrageously expensive restaurants in town for me to buy his dinner. He was an important client from a major airline, and would probably be on his third Glenfiddich by the time I got to the table. Sure enough, Howard looked slightly wobbly as he stood to shake hands.

"How's the family?" he asked.

"Lisa's pregnancy is complicated. We'd appreciate your prayers."

"Will do, Tommy. You know, Dorothy and I are expecting our

first grandchild in January."

"That's great, Howard. Congratulations."

"Let's get a big old juicy steak before we have to talk business," Howard announced. He rubbed his ample belly. "I've been waiting for this all day."

"Sounds good," I scanned the menu and tried not to cringe. Forty five dollars for prime rib?

"Good evening, Mr. Robinson," the waiter appeared suddenly at my elbow. "Would you like to begin with a cocktail? May I suggest an appetizer? We have an excellent selection."

I glanced at Howard and knew he was beef-ready and disinterested in ahi tuna or bacon-wrapped scallops. "I'll have what's he's having, plus a glass of ice water, please. We'll order when you get back."

"Yes, sir."

Howard's cell phone rang and he excused himself. I looked around the dining room. Posh. Chandeliers and burgundy carpet. Tall candles and fresh roses on each table. We had a view of Lake Shore Drive and the Chicago River, a scene I never tired of watching. There was a couple holding hands further down the window, engrossed in conversation. The woman's hair was dark and twisted into a high bun. The back of her black dress was slit dramatically to the top of her butt. She had creamy skin with shoulder blades like tiny angel's wings and was leaning dangerously forward toward her date, risking a major wardrobe malfunction.

Howard slipped back into his seat. "Sorry about that. Dorothy was mad because I didn't call when I got to the restaurant."

I smiled. "She still loves you after all these years."

"I don't know about that. I think she loves my free air travel better than anything. Got me talked into a trip to the French Riviera next month."

"I've heard it's beautiful."

"Dorothy wants to sun herself in style before the grandbaby gets here. Says we're not going to travel much after the princess arrives. Our guest room closet looks like a Pepto-Bismol factory exploded in there."

"So you know it's a girl. Lisa and I had CVS done, but we told the doctor we want to be surprised."

"You have a daughter, right? She must be a teenager by now."

"Delaney is twelve going on twenty-five."

"Bet she's thrilled about having a brother or sister."

"Well, she's excited, but really doesn't know what to expect. She's used to being our center of attention, and is the only grandchild on my side."

"Aww, she'll be fine. We have five girls, you know. Big sisters can be a huge help, when they're not tearing each other's hair out. Our youngest starts at Wellesley in a few weeks and Dorothy is beside herself. Wants to go with her."

The waiter placed crystal glasses carefully before me. "Would you gentlemen care to order now?" he asked. He held an iPad-looking gadget at the ready, smiling broadly in anticipation of a big tip. I wondered how long he'd been forced to wear a tuxedo every night and look like he enjoyed it.

"I'll have the New York Strip rare and a lettuce wedge with your house dressing. Baked potato with everything you can pile on it."

"Sounds perfect to me," Howard said. "I'll have the same. Very rare."

The waiter nodded and padded off silently.

"Did you see the babe sitting by the window?" Howard asked. "Her date looks a lot like Pete Darling."

"Who is Pete Darling?" I replied.

"He's on Forbes Top 100 list. Some kind of pipeline company billionaire. Never married. Has a Gulfstream, I think, but he flies with us sometimes."

"Hmm. You're talking about the one sitting with Miss Danger Dress?"

"Yep," Howard said. "I wish she'd lean forward a tiny bit more."

He glanced over his shoulder. "Looks like a movie star or something. Maybe it's that Megan Fox." He looked back again. "I wish she'd get up and walk. You should see her."

"I have a gorgeous pregnant woman at home, Howard. I don't need to see her."

"Well I do, buddy. I need another Scotch, too." He rattled the ice cubes in his glass and attempted to extract the last drop of liquid. "I wish Leonard had noticed."

"Leonard?"

"The waiter. He's trying to break into improv comedy in the Windy City. You ought to talk to people more, Tommy."

"I guess I should. I'm going to hit the men's room before our food gets here. Be right back. Have Leonard bring me another drink too, will you?"

"Sure thing. Check out that woman and tell me if she's Megan Fox."

"Okay, Howard."

As I neared the Darling table, a realization dawned on me. It was my first trip to Illinois since dispatching Kara to her new job, and the woman's back bore a mole in the precise spot I remembered. I made brief eye contact with a clearly startled Kara Lee Evans as I hurried past.

I killed ten minutes in the men's room, hoping they'd be gone when I was forced to walk back. Kara was waiting for me and stood to offer an air kiss. I inhaled her trademark Must de Cartier and tried to block the memories it evoked.

"Tommy Robinson, how are you? Meet my fiance, Pete Darling."

Pete rose awkwardly and shook my hand. "Will you join us? Kara's told me all about you and your kindness to her."

I met Kara's raised eyebrow. "I have to get back to a business dinner. Maybe we could chat another time."

Kara was tugging at her earring and it fell into her crème brulee. I noted a huge diamond on her left hand as she retrieved it.

I couldn't resist. "Pete, here's my card. Give me a call sometime.

It would be nice to get to know you." Maybe it was the scotch, but I was enjoying Kara's nervous squirming tremendously.

"Alabama, huh? I'll be in Birmingham in a couple of weeks. Maybe we could meet for dinner. I have a couple of favorite restaurants in Mountain Brook."

Kara fidgeted with her napkin and delicately blotted her lipstick. Next she'd be smoothing her hair, wishing she could make her bun into a ponytail.

"Sounds good, Pete. Nice to meet you. Like I said," I paused dramatically, "call me sometime."

Kara looked like she might throw up. I nodded at her, waved goodbye and walked away with a grin.

"Well, is it Megan Fox?" Howard demanded.

"No. It's a woman who used to work for my company. She may look good, but she's not a very nice person. Had to let her go." I gulped my drink and savored the burn as it reached my stomach.

Howard swiveled for one last glance. "If you say so," he mumbled. "Looks like a nice lady to me. Maybe she'll stop on her way out and you can introduce me."

"That's the least likely thing she'll do, trust me."

A group of three people arrived with our dinners and served them elaborately. I stifled a laugh as the third, a teenage boy, bowed slightly at Howard as he left the table.

Leonard appeared at my right. "Will you need anything else, Mr. Robinson?"

Howard shook his head 'no' and I saw he was already chewing vigorously.

"I think we're fine, thank you."

Two and a half hours, two hundred and six dollars later, I hailed a taxi with a signed contract in hand. I noted a shy-looking American driver with relief and closed my eyes to nap on the way to the hotel.

Lisa answered on the first ring. "Hey," she whispered.

"Hey yourself. Everything all right there?"

"We're doing great. You sound tired, babe," she said.

"It's been a long night. Howard sends his best. They signed up for two more years."

"That's wonderful!"

"Yes, it is. I love you, Lisa. See you tomorrow."

"Good night, babe. I love you, too."

Peter F. Darling was true to his word and called on a Friday afternoon.

"Hey, I'm in town and wondered if you'd like to grab some barbecue," he began.

I got up and closed my office door. "I wish I could, Mr. Darling, but my daughter has a dance class and I'm in charge. My wife is on bed rest. We have a baby due in December."

"Some other time, then." Pete paused. "Look, there are some things I should tell you. I think I have some idea why you wanted me to call."

This should be interesting.

"I know a lot more about Kara than you might expect, Mr. Robinson. Okay if I call you Tommy?"

"Of course." I drummed my fingers on the desk.

"I felt like a warthog being seduced by an exotic leopard from the time I met her, and I'm not a very trusting man by nature. In my position, I have investigators at my disposal. I'm not stupid." He sighed. "I know about Boeing and Craig Sanders. I have a pretty good idea what Kara did to you, too. I'm still going to marry her."

"Really?" I didn't know what to add at this point.

"I have never wanted children, and had a vasectomy at forty. She's aware of that as well as the consequences of an 'accidental' pregnancy. My entire estate is willed to my relatives and a number of charities. We have an ironclad prenuptial agreement. Anything less than twenty years, and Kara leaves with nothing but the assets she brought to the marriage. I gave her a very fancy Cartier ring, but that's the extent of it. I'm a frugal man. We plan to live on my ranch in Oklahoma. Simple and private."

"That doesn't sound like Kara." I opined.

"No, I suspect it doesn't. She is willing to agree to those terms, however, to be Mrs. Peter F. Darling. I get a beautiful woman to accompany me when I choose and greet me at the end of a long day when I don't. She *does* know how to welcome a man." He cleared his throat. "I have bodyguards who accompany my fiancee and will continue to do so throughout our years together. They are women I trust."

"Women?"

"Oh yes. Like I said, I'm not stupid, Tommy."

I found that debatable but said, "Well, congratulations and best wishes to you both."

"Thank you. Best of luck with your new baby. Maybe we can get together another time."

"Maybe," I responded. "Good luck to you, too. Bye, Pete."

"Bye."

She's Back

Tommy

Her perfume entered my office before she reached the door, instantly churning the tuna sandwich and potato chips I'd just finished into a major stomach storm. I reached for my antacids as she purred, "Hi, Tommy."

"Why are you here, Kara?" She was tanned and leaner than ever, wearing a low-cut white sundress instead of her usual black on black. Her hair was long and loose, swept off her face by some five hundred dollar Ray Bans. Gorgeous as always, flashing me a cheerful smile. I hated my eyes for traveling to her boobs and my body for its reaction.

She deposited herself into a chair and tugged at the strap of her stiletto. I noticed her trademark red toenails were now a demure pink. The blushing bride.

"I need to talk to you for a few minutes. I can only get away from Butch and Butcher for so long." She swept her hand toward my window. "Take a look. They're my new companions. I escaped by showing them my old company ID and telling them security would require they wait outside. I'm sure they'll amuse themselves by tipping cars or killing stray animals with their bare hands."

I spotted two burly women standing next to an Escalade limo, scanning my company's parking lot. "Nice to see you're not lonely, Kara. What the hell do you want?"

"I know what you told Pete about me and how you tried to sabotage our marriage," she began, "but you failed, Tommy. We'll be making things legal in three weeks. Pity you can't join us in Paris, but you can read all about it in the society pages." She reached over to pick up a photo of Delaney from my desk. "My, she is growing up so fast. I'll never get to have children, and it makes me sad."

"You'd be the kind of mother who would eat her young, Kara."

She chuckled and replaced the picture frame gently. "Probably. Anyway, when we saw you in Chicago I knew you were going to cause problems for me. I'm here to discuss the fallout."

"What does that mean?"

"It seems that my fiance has crafted a prenup that makes the Great Wall of China look like a picket fence. I can become Mrs. Peter F. Darling, Billionaire, but I don't get much of his money and I have to travel with the Bulgarian wrestlers you saw out there, all thanks to you and your meddling."

"I didn't tell him anything he didn't already know."

"Bullshit."

"He was smart enough to check your past on his own, Kara. Ask him."

"He would never have done that, Tommy, unless you told him to. He's been a swooning, puppy-eyed, obsessed man from the moment we happened to meet and discover our shared passions." She arched a perfect brow for emphasis and nibbled at her bottom lip. "I am going into this marriage with a joyful heart and an empty pocketbook. I have no real assets, Tommy, and you are going to remedy that."

Not this again. I rounded the desk and grabbed her arm. "Get out, Kara. Now."

"Take your damn hand off me," she growled. "Pete's in Atlanta and I told him I was coming over here to say hello while he's in meetings. I'm officially conferring with you on a software issue. Isn't that cute? I'm helping you with programming for old times' sake."

She was at least half a mile past crazy and entering certifiably insane territory. I was trying hard to think of a way to get her out of my office. We often had no security at lunchtime. Of course, she'd known that.

"Anyway," she continued, "I am here to make arrangements for the transfer of Aviation Systems ownership you owe me. Twenty percent is perfect."

"You are truly out of your mind."

"Am I? You shattered my heart, Tommy. I cried for weeks after I left here. I wanted to die. I began a new life and found someone who cares about me, but you went and tried to ruin *that*. You're lucky I don't demand more."

"Kara, what you're talking about is impossible. It is not going to happen."

"I beg to differ." She smiled and her eyes flashed deadly sparks at me. "Is Lisa still in the hospital or at home?"

Oh, God.

"Answer me. I am concerned about her and the baby. I heard she's having complications." She was grinning, or maybe just baring her teeth.

"Lisa is none of your business, Kara. Neither am I."

"Oh, but you are. I've been thinking about this for a while now. I don't want to cause your wife any stress at this" —she cleared her throat—"difficult time. But since you tried to poison Pete against me, I feel I have no choice."

I walked to the door, trying to appear confident. My body was rapidly dissolving into jelly. "Get out. Last warning."

"Oh, what are you going to do? Call the police and tell them a lady is threatening you? Security won't be back for twenty minutes. My lady escorts don't care if you run out of here screaming with your hair on fire. As a matter of fact, I could tell them you threatened *me*. They know how to bring a man to his knees in three seconds flat. That would be really embarrassing in your parking lot."

"Stay away from my family."

"I wish I could promise that, Tommy, but I think your spouse deserves the truth as much as mine. I'm every bit as pure in intention as you were."

"The devil is purer in intention than you, Kara."

"That is unkind, to say the least. I was very good to you in so many ways, baby, don't you remember?" She dug in her handbag to produce a card, then laid it carefully next to Delaney's sixth grade portrait. "Mail the paperwork to this address within two weeks. Sorry for the rush, but we need to complete our business before the wedding." She smirked and peered out the window at her bodyguards, now perched on the Cadillac's back bumper with cigarettes. "Those two don't like to shop at all. It's a shame. I could do a hell of a makeover on them."

"When is this lunacy going to stop? I promise you, I'll die before I'll sign an Aviation Systems paperclip over."

"You know enough about me to figure out what an empty threat that is, Tommy." She picked up her handbag and swung it to her shoulder. "Nice chatting with you. I'll be back to see your lovely wife if I don't get my present in the mail. I sure hope she's feeling strong enough for a visit. Girl talk can be exhausting." She rolled her eyes. "I've always preferred the company of men. Good thing my companions are hybrids of some sort."

"Kara, this is blackmail. It's illegal . . ."

"Of course it is. Feel free to call the local authorities. My life is an open book and your chapters are especially juicy. I should probably write them down," she paused thoughtfully and added, "Don't even think of contacting Pete, either. That would make me angry." She pawed through her purse again, making sure I saw her pistol. "I feel so much more secure carrying my own weapon. My ladies-in-waiting are more babysitters than protectors, you know?"

I opened my office door and checked the hallway. It was empty. "Leave, Kara. Now."

"I want to say hello to my former colleagues."

"No. Even you must realize they hated you. Are you oblivious to the way others perceive your act?"

"I didn't burn any bridges here, Tommy. Not even the ones with filthy, slimy water flowing underneath." She licked her thumb and swiped a crumb from my cheek. "You're a mess, baby. Looks like you've added twenty pregnancy pounds."

"Get out," I hissed through clenched teeth.

"Okay. I'll look forward to my wedding gift." She turned back and winked as she reached the door. I watched her rejoin her entourage and climb into the limo, no doubt preparing to pour herself a glass of champagne. When the taillights were out of sight I collapsed and tried to concentrate on my afternoon schedule. Three meetings and a video conference at four o'clock should distract me from the latest missile Kara had fired. After that, I had no idea what I'd do.

The horrible, excruciating path was the only one in sight.

"Mom? I need to talk to you tonight. Mind if I stop by on the way home?"

"Sure. Is Lisa all right?"

"Yes, she's in bed. Delaney was dropped off by a friend's mom, so she's there taking care of her."

"I'll look for you soon, then. I'm cooking pork chops, mashed potatoes and gravy."

My stomach clenched in anticipation. I grabbed some Tums and headed to my truck.

"Your father's still upstairs napping," she whispered as she let me in. We can talk in the kitchen. Want a cold beer?"

"Do you have anything stronger?"

She gave me her startled owl look and turned toward the liquor cabinet. "Scotch?"

"Yes, please. Just a few ice cubes."

Mom had already put an assortment of cheeses and crackers out. When she joined me with her wine I cleared my throat and began, "I have to tell you something. It's bad. You may not forgive me, but you're the only person I can turn to for help."

By the time I'd described the way I met Kara at the shooting range and most of what followed, her glass was empty. My mother did something she'd never done: she slapped my face. Hard. I sat and rubbed my cheek as she poured herself a fresh dose of Chablis.

I steeled myself for the words. They would be worse than any slap.

"What the hell were you thinking? Of course, you *weren't* thinking. You have a beautiful and gracious wife, a perfect and loving daughter. You were taught right from wrong. God, Tommy, I'm glad your Mama D. never had to know this. I wish I didn't." She jumped up to turn the stove off and sat back down. "I can't begin to tell you how disappointed I am in you. Your father cannot hear a word of this. It would kill him." She paused for breath and continued, "Why are you confessing your story to me? Why now?"

"Because she's threatening to tell Lisa."

Her eyes rolled heavenward and returned to mine. "You are an idiot, son."

"I know. I *know*. It never occurred to me I was setting myself up for blackmail. I made a mistake . . . ."

"Putting a postage stamp upside down on an envelope is a mistake. Mashing the wrong elevator button is a *mistake*. Don't trivialize what you've done." She slapped my other cheek with more gusto this time. I was wondering if I'd be sent for a switch from the weeping willow out back. A rush of memories: stealing Jimmy Willingham's catcher's mitt when I was nine . . . forging Mom's signature to get out of a P. E. class in tenth grade . . . dropping a lit joint on her prized sofa and turning the cushion over to hide it . . .

"Don't say another word," she ordered. "Answer these questions. Will she call Lisa? Is she coming in person?"

"Our home phone is disconnected in the bedroom, and she couldn't get Lisa's cell number. I think she plans to come to the house. I have two weeks before she'll be here. *If* she shows up." I rubbed my sore face. "She seems to know about the problems with the pregnancy, and," I added miserably, "realize I can't move my wife out of the house. In any event, she is giving me two weeks to meet her demands."

"I'll start staying with Lisa every day in a week or so, until you get home in the afternoon. Your dad can manage without me." She frowned. "This is the dark-haired one I met at your Christmas party, right?"

"Yes."

"I cannot believe this. I simply can't imagine what possessed you. Yes, I can." She hit the table in exasperation, then patted her hair into place reflexively to regain her composure, sighing, "Do you think Lisa suspects anything?"

"No."

"This woman is crazy enough to extort you. Do you think she might harm you, Lisa or Delaney physically? You said she is an expert with a gun."

I shifted in my chair, squirming as she ladled on more guilt and worry. "I don't think so, Mom. Kara is on the verge of marrying her wealthiest prospect to date. She wouldn't jeopardize that."

My mother crossed her arms over her chest and leaned back, shifting into planning mode. I'd seen her do it a thousand times in various crises. Usually they'd involved my youthful stupidity; now we'd graduated to the middle-aged version.

It was as though she read my mind. "At least you didn't buy a tiny red sports car. We should get "Cliche" tattooed on your arm. Maybe your forehead."

Sarcasm was a good sign. My scotch was gone and I asked, "Mind if I go refresh my drink?"

"No. I would if I were you." She dismissed me with a perfect eye roll.

Dad started down the stairs as I closed the cabinet.

"Hey, Tommy! Get another glass and I'll join you. Are we celebrating?" He rubbed his eyes. "I could use some good news. Damn back's been bothering me all day."

"No, Dad, not celebrating. Just unwinding and visiting my parents." I poured his and offered it as we headed to the kitchen. Mom instantly sat up straight and put on her prettiest smile.

"Pork chops will be a while. I got lost in conversation with Tommy. Have some cheese and crackers, honey."

"Don't mind if I do," Dad replied, grabbing a handful of snacks.

I felt lower than a subterranean termite at the bottom of the Grand Canyon and sat twirling my glass around, staring at it.

"What's wrong, son?" Dad asked. "Is there something new with Lisa and the baby?" He glanced at Mom.

"No, Dad. Just a bad day in the office."

"You read about Saban's new recruit?"

"No, I am way behind on football, Dad. Tell me."

"Alabama is looking real strong again this year. They're going to need a bigger trophy room. I'm hoping you and I can get to a game or two if," he paused and tapped his finger on the table, "if, you know, Lisa and the baby are doing well."

My mother cleared her throat and returned to the stove. "I'll finish supper while you two visit. Why don't y'all move your snacks to the living room? I've had enough man talk for a while." She glared at me and reached for a saucepan, making as much clatter as she could and using way more force than necessary to put it on a burner.

Dad shuffled after me to the couch and sat his drink on his belly.

"You look sunburned, buddy," he observed. "Been stealing time away from the office to fish?"

"No," I rubbed my cheek. "I guess I've been by the pool too much."

"Hmm. Too much sun is a bad thing. I wish I could keep your mom out of the garden."

"Yeah."

Dad and I chatted about sports, his insurance worries and the depressing stock market for forty-five long minutes. I excused myself to call and check on Lisa and Delaney.

"She's asleep, Daddy. Beastie and I are watching tv. I ate some chicken casserole and the last of Grandma's pound cake. Will you ask her to send more if she has any?"

"Sure, baby. Make sure the doors are locked. Why aren't you doing homework?"

"I'll start it soon. I only have a little reading and some math."

"Okay. I'll be there in an hour or so."

"All right, Daddy. Everything's under control here."

My sweet and ever-responsible daughter. I cleared my throat to steady my voice. "Umm, Delaney, if there are any calls from numbers you don't recognize, don't answer. The phone in our room is unplugged so your mom can rest."

"Okay. Stupid telemarketers. Got it."

If only. "Thanks. I'll go ask about that pound cake before I forget. I love you."

"Love you too, Daddy."

An hour later Mom escorted me to the door with Delaney's cake wrapped in foil. "Tommy, if I ever again hear about you being involved with another woman, I will be the one to tell your wife. Do you understand me?"

"Yes, ma'am." I studied the worn carpet.

She tilted my chin up with her index finger for the thousandth time in my life. "I love you, son."

"I love you, too, Mom." Her hug was warm and forgiving enough to bring tears to my eyes, making the night sky a brilliant white blur as I glanced up and whispered a prayer of thanks for my family.

The Plan

Ellen

I watched a black Escalade pull to the curb in front of Tommy's house. Two big women got out and opened the door for Kara, elegant in a sleek brown silk suit and stilettos. Her hair was swept into a chignon—pure movie star. She carried a gift wrapped in pink and blue ribbons and conferred briefly with her escorts, peeling bills from a large roll and handing two to each of them. One nodded in agreement as the taller guard eyed the living room window, catching sight of me. I waved at her but she seemed not to notice. They sped off a few seconds later, leaving their charge standing on the sidewalk. I hurried to flip a switch and press a button, then opened the door before she could ring the bell and wake Lisa.

"Hello, Mrs. Robinson," she cooed. "I met you at an Aviation

Systems Christmas party. Nice to see you again."

"And you, Kara. Please come in." I waved her to the couch facing the fireplace and took a seat to her right.

"I can only stay a little while," she began nervously, "my security guards are on a brief errand. Just wanted to deliver this baby gift to Lisa and say hello."

"I'm afraid she's resting, but I'll be sure to give it to her."

Her eyes traveled to the mirror above the fireplace, reflecting the stairs. "I don't think she'd mind if I wake her. Lisa was kind enough to secure a job for me in Chicago, and I'd like to thank her properly." This was followed by a saccharine smile.

"That's enough, Kara. I know why you're here. I've heard all about you and Tommy, unfortunately. You are not going up those stairs, but you're welcome to sit with me until the ladies return for you." Shock and disappointment skittered across her features, leaving her face looking like I'd just fed her a bite of bell pepper pudding.

"Did he tell you we were in love?" She sighed heavily and leaned back, crossing her arms defensively.

"No, he didn't. This, Kara, means love," I pointed to the worn gold band on my finger. "Your time with Tommy would be better represented by a black lace thong."

She laughed softly. "Maybe so. It's ancient history now. I've moved on."

"I heard. Congratulations on your engagement."

Kara regarded her diamond ring with a smile. "I made a special trip to deliver this gift, Mrs. Robinson. I'm going to take it to Lisa and then I'll wait out front for my ride."

"No, you won't."

She stood and I rose with her, careful to place myself properly in her path. Kara paused for a few seconds, then responded by reaching into her handbag and producing a gun.

"Please move so I can visit Lisa."

I stayed in place and threw my hands into the air. "Are you

threatening to shoot me, Kara?"

"Not at all." The pistol remained out, but she didn't point it at me.

"That's what you'll need to do to get up those stairs." I smiled sweetly at her, and she inched her aim upward in my direction, her dark eyes locked on mine.

"Just move, Mrs. Robinson. I have no desire to harm an old lady."

"That won't be necessary, Kara. You've done quite enough already. There are two cameras in this room, and you've done a superb job of waving your weapon at me. In addition, you were captured from the front door paying your security escorts off."

She shoved the gun back into the handbag, her eyes darting around the room.

"I promise you won't find the cameras, Kara. They are well hidden."

"I don't believe you," she answered, "you're bluffing."

"I never lie, Kara. If you push your luck, you'll find that your fiance and father will receive DVD copies of your performance by tomorrow afternoon. I think you'd have a hard time explaining your actions, don't you?"

She sank back onto the couch to think.

"Here is what you are going to do, Kara. You will hand me that baby gift with a brilliant smile for your finale. Then you'll walk to the front door and wait for your keepers outside. You will never come near my son or his family again, because if you do, I will personally ensure the destruction of your life as Mrs. Peter F. Darling."

She examined the manicured hands in her lap.

"In addition," I continued, "you are going to leave your pistol here with me."

"I sure as hell will not," she hissed.

"By the way, Tommy knows you're here. He programmed my phone with a text to alert him when you drove up." I added casually, "Would you like a Coke or something? He should be here any minute."

She shot her eyes to the window anxiously.

"You can wait by the curb. The trash cans are out there today. You'll fit right in." I held out my hand. "The pistol, Kara."

"It's leaving with me, Mrs. Robinson."

"All right then. It's evidence whether you have it or I do, I guess." I shrugged my shoulders. "I'm not used to being threatened with guns, especially not during social visits." I waved a hand toward the door. "It's time for you to go."

"He actually told you about us? His own *mother*?" Her brows narrowed to bracket a tight, wrinkly gap. I noted the lines with satisfaction.

"Yes, he did." I took a deep breath of Cartier perfume and nearly gagged. "Tommy can't change the past, but we have some control over the future now. Thanks for performing so well on video." I crossed to open the door as he sped into the driveway. "Oh, look. My son's home. I'm sure he'd like to speak with you before you go."

She snatched up the baby gift and stalked out. I saw Tommy jump from his truck, pointing to the street angrily. Kara threw the fancy box to the ground and delivered the third facial slap he'd received this month.

They were gesturing wildly and I hoped the neighbors weren't around. We had about half an hour before Delaney would be dropped off. Surely Kara would be gone by then.

I heard Lisa calling me. The stairs were easy with my adrenaline rush.

"Who was that?" she asked, pulling herself into a sitting position.

"Some girl selling magazines. I told her you don't need any." I was afraid she'd get up and go to the window, so I deposited myself next to her on the side of the bed. "How are you feeling?"

"Disgusting. All I do is eat and sleep." She brushed her hair back carefully and focused on the bathroom door. "Could you give me a hand?"

I helped Lisa off the bed and watched her slowly maneuver her way in and close the door. I crossed to the front window and parted the thick curtains. Kara was standing near the street, tapping her toe impatiently and talking on her cell phone. My son was nowhere in sight, though his truck was still there. He came into view as the Cadillac rounded the corner. The Amazons got out and ushered Kara into the car. Once she was secured, Tommy approached the driver. He spoke to her briefly and closed the door after she climbed in, tapping the roof in farewell. I noticed he was taking pictures with his phone as they pulled away.

Lisa eased herself back into bed. "A girl selling magazines, huh?"

"Well . . ." I began.

"I saw her from my window, Ellen," she interrupted. "We should probably talk about it." She patted the bed and I returned to her side. "Why the hell was she here?"

"To deliver a baby gift to you. Tommy has it."

She sighed wearily and arranged her gown over the mountainous baby bump. "I am not buying that for a minute, Ellen. Kara Evans would be more likely to gain fifty pounds and give up her make-up than do anything nice for me."

"I don't know what to say, Lisa."

"Ellen," she began, "I suspected Kara was after Tommy from the minute I met her. Honestly, I'm not even sure I cared that much. Our marriage had been in trouble for a long time." She paused and looked toward the window. "We went for almost a year without any sort of intimacy. I had the world's longest headache." Her mascara was tracking her cheeks and she reached for a tissue. "I kept smelling her perfume on his clothes," her voice cracked, "and I planned to follow him one day, but I chickened out." She regarded the ceiling and chuckled, post-persimmon style. "My response was to try to lure his attention back, and it wasn't going well. Then I found out I was pregnant." She was sobbing into the tissue and I handed her another. "The next thing I knew, he was asking me to call and get her a job with a friend's company in Chicago. Tommy said she had 'boyfriend trouble'. I set things up for her with Clarke and never mentioned to my husband I was pretty sure *he* was the boyfriend." Lisa was shredding the used tissues into tiny bits, making a neat pile of regrets on her bedside table.

"Shouldn't you be telling him all of this, honey?"

"I don't know, Ellen. I would want to wait until the baby's safely born. I know I can't discuss any of it with him until then. It's too much . . ."

Tommy cleared his throat from the bedroom doorway and triggered a full avalanche of sobs from his wife. I noticed his reddened cheek had an Iron Eyes Cody tear of its own and hoped my son was capable of extricating himself from the quagmire he'd created. I nodded to him as I approached the door and said, "I'll go make a snack for Delaney and give you two some privacy."

"Thanks, Mom." Tommy stepped up to the noose.

Telltale Heart

Abby

Folsom Middle School was rebuilt and ready for fall of 2011. The lobby featured a portrait of "Mr. Will" Santos, lost in April's storm, along with a plaque rededicating the building. My classroom had a lovely view of the outdoor lunch area; once populated by murderous live oaks, it was now bare earth and brightly colored plastic tables.

I was teaching English to seventh and eighth graders this year, most of whom I knew well. They were transformed by a traumatic spring and summer, refreshingly subdued and respectful. Five weeks in, I'd managed to cover more material than had taken two months before. I was sure they still called me "Blabby Abby" and did my best to earn the title.

My favorite class was last period, as the day wound down and the more astute older kids filed in. We were studying *The Telltale Heart*. Not one student appreciated Mr. Poe as much as I, but they paid good attention and showed signs of occasional interest.

A knock at the door interrupted my opening questions. A man entered carrying a huge bouquet of red roses, causing sighs and giggles to frolic through the room. It wasn't my birthday, and I was intrigued enough to pause and open the card. It was signed, "Will." I didn't know a Will, and thought maybe there had been a mix-up. I'd call the florist after class.

Jimmy Ledbetter and Derek Trueblood had incited a minor riot at the back of the first row while I wasn't looking. I slammed my palm on the blackboard and whispered, "Quiet." I had discovered whispering was more effective than yelling. Order was restored after three more glares at the culprits.

"So, as I was saying, what does the narrator want us to believe about him?"

Delaney Robinson raised her hand. "That he is not crazy?"

"Good, Delaney. Can someone else tell me what the narrator despised about the old man?"

Silence.

"You all *did* read this last night, correct?"

More silence. Delaney, my self-appointed assistant, turned and scanned the row behind her. "I did," she offered proudly.

"Anyone else?"

Something was up. Two girls who normally competed for my attention sat giggling and staring at their desktops.

I cleared my throat and resumed, "What is the task the narrator undertakes?"

Molly and Cheyenne continued to smile vacantly. I would have sworn they were glancing nervously at the door, watching for action in the hall.

"Molly?"

"He kills the guy."

"That's correct."

As if on cue, Cheyenne handed Molly a note. I was appalled she didn't even try to hide it and marched over to grab the tiny piece of paper.

"You" was all it said. "We will discuss this after class, girls," I said. I put the note on my desk and tried once more to regain control.

"How did the police know to come to the old man's house?"

I was facing a group of grinning garden gnomes, none of whom raised a hand.

I collapsed into my chair. "Enough. All of you can spend the next twenty minutes doing what I asked you to do last night. I'm disappointed in you." They dutifully turned to reading, or pretending to read. I opened my laptop and checked my email. There was a sale at Macy's. I was qualified for penile enlargement.

I jumped when Luke burst into the room, afraid Faith had come to check on me and I was busted. I shot him a look of annoyance. He knew better than to interrupt.

"This will just take a minute," he said. "I need to borrow your electrical outlet. Mine are still messed up." All eyes followed Luke as he produced an iPod and hooked up a couple of small speakers on the shelf by the window. He turned to Delaney and nodded. She went to the light switch and darkened the room slightly. Luke produced a small video camera and handed it to Jimmy. *What in the world . . .*

My boyfriend gave me a coy smile as the music started. "Marry Me" by Train.

I froze, trying to process. "Will. You. Marry Me."

"Luke . . ."

"What? They all think it's a good idea." He waved at the class, now completely dissolved into laughter and applause.

I crossed to him and did the only thing that made sense. "Yes," I told him, tears streaming down my face.

"Good, because otherwise this would be really embarrassing." Delaney jumped up and handed Luke a little black box. He opened it and slid a brilliant square diamond onto my shaking finger.

"I expect y'all to dance at our wedding," Luke announced. "Miss Ferguson, is that all right with you?"

I nodded, numb. Did he just invite thirty students to a wedding I hadn't begun to plan?

Faith came hurrying in with a white sheet cake and deposited it on my desk, holding her right hand high to prevent a stampede. My own telltale heart pounded in my ears as I watched Delaney go to the closet and extract a bottle of apple juice and some plastic cups. Our assistant principal, Mrs. Dryden, appeared with plates and forks.

"Abby, don't tell the school board I allowed a party in this pristine classroom, all right?" Faith intoned. She waved cheerfully at the first row of desks.

The kids jumped up and formed an orderly line to the refreshments. I chose that moment to offer a quick kiss to my fiance's cheek and whisper, "What took you so long?"

Luke chuckled and traced my jawline with his finger. "Had to get clearance from my folks to marry a Yankee."

"Bless your heart," I responded, turning my eyes to the ceiling. "You get bonus points for originality."

"I could have gone with a flash mob at tonight's football game. That was Plan B."

"Color me grateful, Mr. Bradley. By the way, did you really invite the entire class to our wedding, or did I imagine that?"

"I thought you'd want a big wedding."

"Well, we've never talked about it, Luke. I might want to get married in my childhood church in Kansas."

"Hmm. We may have to have two weddings. Do they make houndstooth bridal dresses?"

"No. They are illegal."

"What about cummerbunds?"

"Illegal as well."

"I guess we need to talk about this wedding planning stuff." He grinned and waved at Delaney, who carried a monstrous slice of cake and settled next to her best friend to chat and giggle.

"There is a lot we haven't discussed, actually."

He eyed me curiously. "Like the fact I want ten children?"

"Not funny. Not funny at all."

Luke scanned the room and found everyone busy eating, so he gave my tummy a furtive pat. "You don't want ten?"

"I don't know if I want more than one. Jeez, Luke, I'm twenty-four. Slow down."

"You are dampening my engagement excitement here, Abby."

I turned and walked away before snapping one of my trademark witty comebacks at him, mostly because I couldn't think of one. Faith motioned me over.

"I am so happy for y'all," she said, hugging me hard. "Here," she handed me a slice of cake, "the lunch ladies baked this for you."

"How long have you known he was going to do this?"

"Since before school started." She frowned. "You *are* happy about it, right?"

"Yes. It's just . . . sudden. I'm still in shock. And Luke's already throwing stuff at me about having babies. Lots and lots of babies." My future husband was fiddling with his iPod. He shot me a defiant look as Carrie Underwood's "American Girl" began playing.

I turned to Faith. "Isn't the noise going to disturb other classes?"

"Nope. The rooms near yours are empty. Field trip, remember?"

"Oh."

"So, how soon do you think the wedding will be?"

"I have no idea." I looked at my glittering ring and smiled at Luke, halfway through his second piece of cake.

"The high school is lucky to have him. I suspect he'll be promoted to head coach before too long," she said.

"What are you talking about?"

"Oh. I'm sorry," Faith sputtered. "Luke should tell you."

"Tell me what?"

"I spoke out of turn, Abby. Ask him about it. I'm going to wrap this party up. Thirty minutes until dismissal." She pointed to the clock and asked for help with clean-up, instantly summoning ten eager-to-please students.

"Class," Faith called, "Let's say Happy Weekend to Miss Ferguson and Mr. Bradley. I'm taking over for the rest of this period. I believe we're studying *The Telltale Heart*?" She nodded at me and I smiled. "We'll see y'all Monday morning."

Luke and I made our exit to a mixed chorus of groans and well wishes. He turned and grabbed the roses, then opened the door for me. As soon as we were out of sight, he kissed me slow and sweet enough to melt my knees. "We have time for you to pack a few things," he whispered. "I'm kidnapping you."

"Pack for what? Where?"

"It's a secret. Plan for anything."

We made our way to his truck. Luke carefully placed the roses on the passenger floorboard and boosted me up. He climbed in, buckled his seat belt, opened the center console and produced a chilled split of champagne and a straw. He popped the cork and handed the bottle to me. "I love you, Future Mrs. Bradley."

"I love you, too. Please tell me where we're going."

"To your apartment."

"And?"

"An undisclosed location. Trust me, Abby." He grinned and started the truck. "You'll like it very much."

"Oh my gosh, I need to call Becca. And my parents."

"Your dad already knows. I'm old-fashioned enough to ask for your hand."

"What did he say?"

"He tried to limit it to your hand. We made a deal. I love, honor and cherish you every day of my life, and he gets ten fine Bradley grandchildren."

"You are hilarious."

"I figure that's why you said yes. Women adore a sense of humor and," he added, reaching into the back seat, "a black Stetson." He adjusted his hat properly and nodded to himself in the rear view mirror. "Right?"

"I love you, Luke." He was the most beautiful man I'd ever seen, much less dated. And now he was going to be my husband. Heartbeats tickled my fingers as I tried to dig the cell phone out of my purse, clumsy with excitement.

"So call and give the world our news. I'll drive."

I was pretty sure the entire bank lobby heard Becca's scream. "Oh my gosh! Really? How big is the ring? Where is he taking you? I want my maid-of-honor dress to be dark red. No, black . . ."

"He wants the bridesmaids in houndstooth." I turned to a laughing Luke.

"Works for me!" Becca yelled. "I love y'all. Have fun. See you Sunday night."

After I shrieked with my mom and dad for three minutes, I asked Luke if I should call his parents.

"I told them I was asking, and I'd call if you said no. Otherwise, they wouldn't hear from us until Monday night, when we're having a celebration dinner. They love you, Abby."

"I love them, too."

An hour later we headed south. I was sincerely hoping Luke knew I wasn't a Panama City Beach kind of girl. He kept the music at full volume and fresh champagne in my hand. Whatever he'd planned, I'd decided I would enjoy it. Unless we were going deer hunting. Was it deer season? No, couldn't be. I closed my eyes and let the bubbles do their work. When I woke we were driving through Mobile's shipyards.

"Will you tell me now?" I asked sleepily.

"There is a city called Fairhope near here. Very artsy—they even have a writers' colony. I thought you'd enjoy it. It's not our exact destination, though." Luke leaned back and stretched his arms, clutching the steering wheel. He was grinning and acting cocky, obviously pleased with his plan. "Are you hungry?"

"Not really."

"By the time we're settled in, you'll be ready for the room service dinner I've arranged."

"Oh, my. I guess that rules out a Motel 6 or moldy Ramada."

"This place is a bit nicer, Abby. Like I said, trust me."

"I do. We are teachers on a budget, though. I'm not expecting the Ritz, Luke. Anywhere with you will be great."

"Abby, you and I haven't discussed finances much." He tapped the dashboard absently and switched lanes, passing a black Porsche. "Middle school math does not a millionaire make, but I was fortunate to graduate UA with no debt. I've been able to save and invest along the way." He sighed. "Plus, the local high school has hired me as assistant varsity football coach part-time. If things work out, I may be teaching there next year and coaching JV. It would be a pretty serious pay increase."

"Wow. That's great, except," I studied his profile, "I've gotten used to stealing kisses in the hall."

"Well, it's not a sure thing. We may be continuing to scandalize Folsom Middle School for years to come."

"I certainly hope so."

Fairhope was exquisite, a flowery jewel of a town with quaint shops. Even the public wastebaskets were immaculate and topped with colorful petunias. We arrived around sunset and Luke turned down a street lined with graceful oaks. We came to a sparkling fountain surrounded by a rose garden and parked. People were milling about everywhere, taking pictures. Beyond the fountain I spotted a long pier.

"Come on. I want to show you something," he said, opening my door with a flourish. "This is a sight you'll want to remember. I've got my camera."

We walked hand and hand to the end of the pier, surrounded by fishermen and children running wildly with ice cream cones. Somewhere in the distance a band was playing seventies music. Luke pointed.

"That's Mobile's skyline across the bay." The evening lights were coming on, twinkling against a vermillion sky. He turned me around to look back. "Those bluffs along the water have amazing houses. If you try real hard, you can see the crowd dancing on the patio in front of one."

"It's beautiful." I leaned in for a kiss, eager to get to our room. "How far from here are we staying?"

"Just a few minutes. We'll come back tomorrow."

"To fish?"

"To make memories, Abby. There's a park nearby you'll love, fantastic restaurants and antique stores, plus a book store tailor-made for you."

"Obviously you've been here before."

"Many times. My mother's parents retired to Fairhope before I was born. They both passed away within months of each other in 2006. Papa died in February, and Nana's heart gave up after that."

"I'm sorry. I remember you telling me you were close."

"Yeah. I'll drive you by their house while we're here." He stared at a ship in the distance. "Nana and Papa Brewer were wonderful people. You would have loved them, and they would have adored you."

"I'm sure that's true. I grew up without knowing my grandparents on either side. I have vague memories of visits, but I was so young when they died."

"Well, you are getting my Bradley grandparents in this bargain," he replied. "Memaw and Pawpaw heartily approve of you. They're coming to dinner Monday night."

"Exactly how many people are showing up for this celebration dinner?" I asked.

He bit his lower lip and raised his eyebrows, a gesture I'd grown to love. "Well, there will be several aunts and uncles, too. I'm from Alabama, Abby; we have family kudzu instead of trees. They are all looking forward to officially welcoming you into the family."

"Hmm. You must have been pretty sure I'd say yes."

"Never doubted it for a second." He winked. "How could you pass this up?" He swept his arms up and down his body.

Luke noticed an older lady approaching and asked if she'd mind taking a few pictures of us.

"I'd be happy to," she responded. "Are y'all newlyweds? Sure looks like it."

"No ma'am," I said. "He just proposed to me."

"Well, bless your hearts. I hope you have a long and happy marriage and ten healthy children."

"Did he pay you to say that?" I shot a look at my fiance.

"No. Y'all are just too pretty not to have a bunch of kids." She posed the two of us in several directions and handed the camera to Luke. "God bless you. My husband and I spent every Friday evening of our lives on this pier until I lost him three years ago. I brought my granddaughter along with me tonight." She waved at a lovely girl with long blond hair walking toward us. "She goes to Auburn."

"War Eagle," Luke responded.

"Are you an Auburn fan?" she asked.

"Absolutely not, ma'am," he smiled. "Thank you for the pictures."

The entrance to the hotel looked like a theme park, all lush landscaping and spotlights. Luke handed a piece of paper to the guard on duty. He checked his records and returned with a parking pass and map. "Welcome, Mr. Bradley. Enjoy your stay."

"We need a map? How big is this place?"

He flicked the overhead light on. "About five or six hundred acres. Just study it and tell me where to go. You're the navigator."

After a series of turns we were greeted by valets and bellmen who swooped in like we were driving a new Bentley instead of a pick-up. My door flew open and Ramon From Argentina extended a hand.

"Good evening, Miss. Welcome to the Grand Hotel." As soon as I was standing, he started grabbing our luggage from the back seat.

"I'll meet you in your room," he added. "Give this slip to the desk."

Luke whisked me into a breathtaking lobby. I couldn't help but wonder how much our weekend was costing him. I'd never been anywhere so plush in my life. I wandered to the fireplace as he registered, taking a cozy seat and people watching. A group wandered by in tuxedos and formal dresses, laughing and clinking champagne glasses.

"We're all set, Abby. Room 332. Shall we?" He offered his arm.

"Yes, Mr. Bradley." I latched onto him and smoothed my skirt, suddenly feeling very dowdy. "Yes, we shall."

"Let's try to beat Ramon to the room," Luke said, producing a ten dollar bill from his pocket. "We don't need to scandalize him."

"Wanna try?" The elevator doors closed as I threw my arms around his neck and my legs around his waist.

"Jeez, Abby, they have cameras in here."

"Really?" I dropped my feet and smoothed my hair. "Let me spruce up a bit." I offered him my brightest smile and grabbed his butt as the elevator dinged for the third floor.

Ramon was waiting at the door, eager to show us around and collect his tip. The room was beautifully and tastefully furnished, and he showed us the balcony with a lake view. I was focused on the king-sized bed with fluffy pillows.

"Will you be needing anything else?" Ramon asked.

"No, thank you very much." Luke handed him the ten and escorted him to the door.

As soon as it closed, I took Luke's shirt off and threw it to a chair. I started unbuttoning his jeans, then ground my pelvis against him.

"Damn. We should get engaged more often," he whispered. "We have forty minutes until room service gets here."

"Perfect," I said as I yanked off his leather belt and snaked it around his waist, pulling him close. I dropped the belt and ran my fingernails up and down the hard muscles of his back. "You are gonna need a sandwich."

"It's Prime Petite Filet Medallions with Truffled Potato Rounds, Candied Dragon Carrots, Seared Foie Gras and a Madeira Demi Glaze, followed by something they call a Chocolate Trilogy. I memorized it."

"I love you more than ever. You are aware that my cooking skills are limited to spaghetti, right?"

"I ain't marrying you for your cooking, honey."

"Well, Mr. Math Major, let me show you how one and one make one." I fell back onto the bed, dragging him on top of me.

We didn't leave our room until Sunday morning, when we greeted the sleepy Fairhope bookstore owner as he opened up. He rubbed his bald head and said, "Welcome. Are y'all looking for anything special?"

"No," I turned to meet Luke's eyes. "We've already found it, thank you."

The Glamorous Life

Kara Lee Evans Darling

There is a delicately framed photo on the fireplace mantle, an ugly split log affair my husband selected to complement his antler décor. Pete and I are forehead to forehead with the glittering Eiffel Tower in the distance at sunset. My hair is arranged in a three hundred dollar tousled updo; his has retreated to the back of his head like Napoleon's troops at Waterloo. The dress was a heavily beaded white Dior I chose for its plunging neckline and forbidden price tag. My husband accessorized his dull, neglected tuxedo with shoes resembling hiking boots.

We had been married for thirty minutes. I was drunk on my new title and French champagne. Pete was complaining about his sore feet after our day-long walking tour and trying to convince me to forget Maxim's and dine in a cheaper restaurant a buddy had recommended near a dingy train station. Seems they had great

Chicago-style steaks.

I made a few honeymoon promises I found thoroughly distasteful to get the ambiance I wanted for our post-nuptial meal. In retrospect, I should have let him take me to a Parisian McDonald's and saved myself a lot of time and trouble in bed.

I knew what he liked and how he liked it. I hadn't planned on his obsession with the Dow and international business news. Sex was scheduled between phone calls about geological problems in the States and marathon viewings of CNN, BBC News and whatever commentary Pete could locate regarding the global economy.

Ah, romance.

According to Pete, the art in the Louvre and Musée d'Orsay was "boring" except for the Mona Lisa and Venus de Milo, and "not worth the admission price." Versailles shocked him with its ostentation. The majestic Notre Dame Cathedral was "musty." Rich French cuisine gave him gas and required an immediate nap. He preferred American wine or beer. Our trip to the top of Tour Eiffel was the only non-sexual highlight for Pete because it reminded him of a Jackie Chan movie.

The City of Light can be seriously dimmed by the wrong travel companion. Mine was a human rheostat, capable of clouding diamonds with his moods. He could remove bubbles from champagne with his mere presence. The locals should have hired him to age cheese.

He'd been romance-challenged from the beginning, an awkward adolescent middle-aged man with beer breath enjoying his public outings with a Playboy centerfold. I'd known that. I'd exploited the hell out of it, in fact. I flirted with his business associates just enough to make him notice their eyes on me. I chose cleavage and stilettos for every occasion. My bras were merciless push-ups. I spent every spare cent I had on lingerie and a personal trainer named Rosie, who was anything but. I worked hard to get the proposal, a Cartier ring, one glorious dress and a trip to Paris. Included in the package was the distracted lard lump I now called "husband."

I was unhappy in my role as pipeline emperor's concubine, looking for new interests beyond feminizing the Oklahoma ranch on a budget. Pete had resumed his intensive travel schedule, leaving me in the care of Gargoylia and Gargolynne.

The three of us were sitting on leather couches I found cringe-worthy. My keepers amused themselves with magazines. I assumed they were geared to wrestling or tractor maintenance, though I hadn't glimpsed a cover. I gazed upon the aforementioned honeymoon photo—Cro-Magnon forehead pressed to freshly Botoxed one—and imagined myself back in Paris as a free woman. Anywhere, actually, as a free woman.

The phone rang and one of the gargoyles jumped to answer.

"He's not in. May I take a message?" she growled. A few seconds passed. I heard her say, "I see. I will contact Mr. Darling immediately and have him return your call."

"What's wrong?" I ventured.

"Nothing, Mrs. Darling. I will contact Mr. Darling and I am sure he will address the situation at hand." She flashed a condescending smirk and entered Pete's uber-private cell number.

The next thing I knew, Pete's voice was screaming loudly enough for me to hear ten feet away. "Get him to the ranch on the next flight. I'll be home by tomorrow."

It did not take me long to assess the situation after turning on the TV. A natural gas pipeline had exploded in New Mexico, killing two children in a nearby daycare center and at least ten adults. Hundreds had been transported to local hospitals. It was a horrific scene being covered repeatedly by CNN, Fox News and network channels.

Guess whose pipeline?

Pete arrived the next morning with roadmap eyes and a terrible temper.

"What are you going to do?" I asked.

"I'm not sure yet. My head engineer on that project is on his way, along with a cadre of defense attorneys. This is big trouble, Kara." With that, he poured himself an uncharacteristic morning bourbon and collapsed on the (unfortunately) leather recliner in our bedroom.

"Pete, are you really that worried?"

"I am way beyond worried. This is comparable to Bhopal. It's a disaster, Kara, on every front." He rubbed his temples. "I could lose everything."

"We could lose everything," I corrected.

"Yes, we." He toasted me with a frown and added, "Welcome to my life, baby. This is the nightmare I've feared since I started the business. The worst case scenario." He closed his eyes. "Two three-year-olds playing outside. Just *gone* . . ."

"It will be all right, Pete," I soothed. I crossed the room and knelt at his clodhopper feet. "I am sure the lawyers will figure it out."

"Glad to have your support, Kara." He gulped the bottom of his drink. "I presume you'll still love me after the trial."

"What makes you so sure there will be a trial?"

"The drug addiction of the crew chief involved, for starters. I should have replaced him."

"Oh my God, Pete."

"Yeah. We have insurance, but it's meaningless. The pipe was not installed properly. Some of the steel straps welded over the pipe joints failed. Every personal injury attorney and environmental group in the country will be all over this." He glanced at my engagement ring, casting rainbows on the wall. "I hope you've enjoyed your brief billionaire status."

"Pete . . ."

"Not now." He rose and stepped around me to refill his glass. "I have to get ready for a meeting with a PR guy in twenty minutes."

"Let me help you."

"There is absolutely nothing you can do other than remain by my side and smile for the cameras. There will be tons of them for a while. Practice your calm, sensitive, supportive wife look."

With that, he closed our bedroom door.

I regarded my fingernails, due for a manicure at one o'clock. I would dress conservatively and don sunglasses for the ride to Tulsa. The gargoyles would protect me. There was nothing to worry about.

At twelve thirty I descended the staircase in a somber black silk pantsuit. The television was blaring news of the presidential campaign and my escorts were engrossed. "It should be Hillary," one of them shouted at the announcer.

"You mean that?" I asked her.

"High time a woman held the office. It's the only way we'll save this country." She hit the remote and stood. "This year is just more of the same testosterone-poisoned posturing. Men are nothing but trouble." She glanced at her cohort. "Right, Ceci?"

I found "Ceci" the most improbable name for the two hundred fifty pound bottle-blond ox she'd addressed. Ceci nodded and adjusted her gun.

"Nothing but trouble. You feelin' all right, Mrs. D? You look a little pale." She ran her eyes from my toes upward, rendering me uncomfortable and self-conscious.

"I'm fine. Let's go."

"Not just yet," Ceci intoned. "There are reporters at the end of the driveway. Mr. Darling asked us to split up and drive his car out first as a diversion, then follow a few minutes later with you hidden in the Cadillac."

"Is that really necessary?"

"Yes, ma'am, it is. The public relations man said we should leave and return that way."

"If you say so. Let's hurry up." I glanced at my cell. "I'll call Imelda and tell her we may be running a bit behind."

I laid down in the back seat, prepared for the news vans and reporters. I had not anticipated the protesters with "PFD PIPELINES KILLS BABIES"signs. People slapped the sides of the Escalade. Ceci gunned the accelerator in response.

"You okay?" She met my eyes in the rear view mirror.

"Sure." I sat up straight and fought the panic pounding in my chest. "Do you think they'll go away?"

"No ma'am. Not until they get what they want."

If I had known how prophetic those words were, I might have jumped out and leaped into Ceci's path, allowing the Goodyears to take me to infinity. Instead, I went to Imelda's Nail Salon to get my talons sharpened in vain.

Two hours later we were greeted by a crowd much larger than we'd left. Ceci phoned Pete, who directed us to turn around and head back to a Tulsa hotel room. The latest news was grim: my husband's company was under federal investigation and indictments were likely. I checked us in as Mrs. Otis Garfield.

After a restless night listening to Bertha Blond and Bertha Butt laugh at mindless sitcoms in the adjoining room, I bypassed the morning news and stuck my head in to inform them we were returning to the ranch. I didn't care what Pete said, I was not going to hide in a hotel room with the monsters in tow.

The number of protesters had doubled and two additional news vans camped near the entrance to our home. The signs had grown even more vitriolic: "NEGLIGENCE IS MURDER! DEMAND JUSTICE!" and "PRAY FOR THE BABIES DARLING TOOK" caught my eye as we forced our way through. A brunette reporter I recognized from the local NBC station banged her microphone on Ceci's window. "Is Mrs. Darling in there? I have only two questions. Please stop the car!"

She was ignored and stood patting her hair into place as we sped off.

Pete was at the kitchen table with four men I didn't recognize. He stood and tried to mask his annoyance at my return. "Gentlemen, this is my wife Kara."

I nodded at them and smiled. "Welcome. If I may be of any help, please let me know. I'll be upstairs."

The tall one in jeans and boots rose from the table. He looked like a beefier cowboy version of Colin Farrell. "Ma'am," he nodded. "I'm Johnny Bible. Mr. Darling and I discussed our approach to publicity and damage control earlier, and I'd like to speak with you about your role."

"Johnny Bible? Seriously?"

"Since the day I was born," he grinned. "I swear I did not invent it for PR purposes. It's a fairly common name where I grew up."

"Where is that, Johnny?"

"Alabama. The northeast part."

"Well, how about that. I used to live there."

Pete was eying us warily. I knew he'd summon The Gorgons to monitor our talk, but I was pretty sure it would still be the highlight of my day. I smoothed my pants, wishing they hadn't stretched and wrinkled during my banishment.

"Give me a few minutes to change and freshen up. I'll meet you in the living room." I nodded at Pete's engineer types and exited, making sure my hips swayed a bit.

Mr. Bible was seated on the couch when I returned in a fresh chocolate brown dress and heels. The giantresses sat anxiously by the front window as though expecting a full-press attack. (Pardon the pun.)

"Thank you for taking the time to talk, Mrs. Darling," he began.

I eased into a chair opposite him. "Please call me Kara. I have plenty of time to talk, as my driveway is currently hosting a protest rally and broadcast media convention. I don't think I'll be going anywhere this afternoon." I sighed delicately. "It would be nice to have the option, though."

He nodded cheerfully. "I will be taking care of that shortly."

"Thank you," I beamed at him and crossed my legs.

"Kara, is there anything at all in your background that might be portrayed negatively by the press?"

Epilogue

July, 2012

Dear Mama D.,

I know I can't mail this, but it helps me sometimes to write to you. I still miss you every day. I thought you would want to know what's going on. I have spent two days sitting in the back of our tiny rental car, listening to Dad gripe about having to drive on the wrong side of the road. We had to stop twice yesterday for sheep to cross in front of us! Their backs were spray painted with splotches of cotton candy pink and blue. Mom says it's the way they keep up with whose sheep are whose around here.

Dad hates the tiny Ford we have. We left the airport in Shannon the morning we landed, very tired and all of us wanting to get to our hotel in Dingle to sleep. We had to pull over after only an hour because a tire was going flat. Daddy jumped out and started kicking the tire and the car, cursing like crazy. Mom told him, "Don't shoot your mule, Tommy." I've heard Grandma Ellen say the same thing to Grandpa when he loses his temper. We got the tire fixed at a gas station, which they call a petrol station. That started a whole bunch of grumbling over the prices. I fell asleep listening to it.

I am going to be stuck in the back seat with Patrick for the next two weeks. He's my new little brother, and smiles most of the time unless he is hungry. When he cries I blow in his mouth to shut him up if no one is looking. He has lots of hair already and big brown eyes. There is a tiny red birthmark on his back shaped like a diamond. It's really freaky.

We named him after your grandfather from Ireland and now we are here. We went to the church today in Old Leighlin, the one in your pictures with Carl! Dad got the key from an old man down the road, and we got to walk around inside. The key was humongous and rusty, and it took Dad about an hour to get it to work. The church is very old. The man says the original building dates back to about the year 1200, and there was a cathedral there before that when Saint Patrick was alive. I don't know if you got to go inside, but it is really pretty. It was cold in there because the whole place is made of stone, and there are stained glass windows that look like paintings of light and color. It was not like our church at home at all. They had a big dish full of water that Mom says is a baptismal font. We sat in the pews and the choir chairs. Mom took a million pictures of Patrick held up by Daddy in front of the windows. I think he sort of smiled in one or two out of the hundred she shot. I almost fell asleep in one of the old pews, staring at the plaques on the floor. I am pretty sure they buried people inside the church.

Daddy said he remembered part of a story you told him about your great-grandmother. He said she was starving to death and stole a diamond to sell to save herself and her family. He thought she hid it in a church. It would be so weird if it was the one we were in!

We walked around outside for a long time looking at the tombstones. Most of them were too old to read and some were falling in, which is really creepy. Mom took even more pictures of Patrick and me on the rock walls around the place. There were sheep all around us begging for food. I gave them pieces of a cereal bar.

There was a tree with pretty pink flowers growing near the cemetery. I stole one and put it in my purse to keep. Mom says I will have to hide it in my suitcase.

Patrick got grumpy and we had to leave and find a place to spend the night. Mom took out the guidebook when we got in the car and started reading to Daddy about a bed and breakfast called Buxton Manor. She went on and on about the "beautiful gardens" and "luxurious rooms" and decided it would be the perfect place to stop. It was not far away, so we headed there.

It was amazing! We drove through huge iron gates like you see in front of mansions in the movies. There was a fountain in front with horses on their back legs surrounding it. Dad left us in the car to check in and came back a few minutes later to start unloading luggage. Mom asked me to carry Patrick.

I have never been so embarrassed! He started screaming like I was torturing him as soon as we walked in the door, fighting me and kicking his legs. The old lady at the front desk stared at us like she wished we would disappear. Mom apologized and took him outside. We watched her walking him around and patting his back, showing him the horse statues and trees and anything she could find to shut him up. He finally laid his head on her shoulder and seemed to fall asleep. When she brought him back in he immediately resumed wailing like a police siren. Mom looked at Dad and he shrugged his shoulders. I could tell the lady wanted us to leave. People in the sitting room were glancing at us and quickly looking away. We were about as popular as fresh plague. Mom nodded at Dad and took Patrick to the car.

He told the lady, "We will look for a different place to stay. My son is not feeling well."

"I see," she said. "Babies don't travel well, do they? Give me one moment to refund your credit card." She turned to look at me. "Your little brother will learn to behave as well as you when he's a bit older, I'm sure."

I didn't say a word. Daddy and I carried our stuff out and found Patrick laughing at Mom making faces at him. We drove to Carlow and checked into a nice hotel with big flower arrangements all over the place and a pretty view of the river.

Mom fed Patrick and put him down for a nap. She and Dad ordered a burger for me and they've left me to watch the baby while they have dinner downstairs. The hamburger tastes powdery and strange. It is horrible. I am probably going to eat grilled cheese sandwiches for the rest of the time we are here, which will get me really fat just in time for school to start.

My old school was destroyed in a tornado and they rebuilt it bigger and better than it was. One of my teachers almost died because she was in her classroom and a tree hit her. She is fine now and getting married to another one of my teachers, which is weird. They used to kiss in the halls when they thought no one could see. His name is Mr. Bradley and he's really nice and cute, too.

We left Beastie with Grandma and Grandpa and I am sure they will have fun with him. Their old dog Annie died a long time ago and I think they should get a puppy. Dad thinks so, too. They are doing well, but I know they miss you a lot. Grandma Ellen made me bring some of my favorite pieces of your jewelry over here. She said it would be kind of like having you come along. We are going to stay in a castle next week and I am wearing your blue crystal necklace with a new black dress for my birthday dinner. Mom says movie stars and even kings have stayed there! The best part is, I get to go horseback riding with Mom and Dad is going to be stuck with Patrick.

Even though it is July it is way cooler here than Alabama. The pastures and trees look about the same except for the rock walls around them. We are going to Kilkenny tomorrow. I love the name Kilkenny! Dad says there is a castle to walk around in and some fun places to shop. I am hoping for a restaurant with good food. You would not believe what these people eat for breakfast! I guess you tried all that stuff when you were here, though. Black pudding is the grossest thing I have ever seen except for some of the diapers Patrick produces.

Dad is fascinated by old graves called cairns and something called dolmen stones. We are going to see one of the biggest ones in Ireland after Kilkenny.

Most people have been super nice. They seem to know we are Americans before we even say hello. I told a man in the hotel my family came from near Carlow and he said, "Are ye now? I thought you were pretty enough to be Irish." Then he winked at me.

Patrick will be awake in a few minutes, so I am going to finish this letter and write in my journal. Mom is making me record each day for my first high school essay. A freshman at last! I wish you could see how grown up I am.

I miss you every minute and always will, Mama D.

Love,
Delaney

St. Lazerian's Cathedral
Old Leighlinbridge
County Carlow
Ireland

Made in the USA
Charleston, SC
11 March 2013